"This community could be your home…"

"I'm going to stay," Jeb said, meaning it. "I'm Amish. I've been an Amish man lost in the world."

"You're not lost anymore," Rebecca replied, her eyes telling him the secrets she couldn't voice.

"No, I'm not alone, but I still have many roads to walk before I can be completely at peace."

"You did talk to the bishop. That is a start."

"It is. I have to let him know if I'm committed. Now, after your words to me, I am committed more than ever."

"I'm glad," she said, her hands clutched over her apron. "I like having you around."

He smiled. "I like being around you, but, Becca, we have to accept that before I can be true, I need to find God again. Then I'll work my way toward the other part of why I'm staying."

"And what would that be?" she asked, her breath held on the air.

"You, Becca," he whispered. "You make me feel this peace inside my soul."

With over seventy books published and millions in print, **Lenora Worth** writes award-winning romance and romantic suspense. Three of her books finaled in the ACFW Carol Awards, and her Love Inspired Suspense novel *Body of Evidence* became a *New York Times* bestseller. Her novella in *Mistletoe Kisses* made her a *USA TODAY* bestselling author. Lenora goes on adventures with her retired husband, Don, and enjoys reading, baking and shopping…especially shoe shopping.

Visit the Author Profile page
at LoveInspired.com for more titles.

Secrets in an Amish Garden

Lenora Worth

LOVE INSPIRED

INSPIRATIONAL ROMANCE

LOVE INSPIRED®
INSPIRATIONAL ROMANCE

Recycling programs
for this product may
not exist in your area.

ISBN-13: 978-1-335-40976-8

Secrets in an Amish Garden

Love Inspired
22 Adelaide St. West, 41st Floor
Toronto, Ontario M5H 4E3, Canada
www.LoveInspired.com

Printed in U.S.A.

Consider the lilies how they grow:
they toil not, they spin not; and yet I say
unto you, that Solomon in all his glory was
not arrayed like one of these. If then God so
clothe the grass, which is to day in the field, and
to morrow is cast into the oven; how much more
will he clothe you, O ye of little faith?
—*Luke* 12:27–28

To my dear editor Patience Bloom
for always helping me through the writing life.
You are the best!

Chapter One

"April showers bring May flowers."

Rebecca Eicher smiled at her seven-year-old niece's solemn statement. "And who told you that, wise little Katie?"

"Daed," Katie said with a snaggle-toothed grin. "He's always telling me things."

"That's what makes *daeds* so special," Rebecca replied. She sure missed her parents, especially during spring. Glancing at the old clock on the kitchen wall, she said, "And it's time for you to run home. Your *mamm* will be wondering if Aunt Becca hid you under a honeysuckle bush."

"I won't fit under a bush," Katie said

with her elbows out and her hands on her blue dress. "I'm getting taller every day."

"You for certain sure are," Rebecca replied as she took Katie's hand and guided her and the bag of snickerdoodle cookies they'd just finished baking toward the front door. "Now, don't run or you'll break all the cookies and then the chickens will peck at them."

"I'll walk really slow," Katie retorted, walking like a creature from the forest, her steps wide and exaggerated.

"Perfect," Rebecca said. "I'll watch you across the road."

"And I'll watch for cars or buggies," Katie said, knowing the rules. "I promise."

Rebecca walked out to the end of the lane with Katie and gave her a kiss. "Okay, run along now, *liebling*."

She loved her freckle-faced golden-haired niece as well as Katie's three older brothers, Michael, Elijah and Adam. Blessed that her own older brother, Noah, and his wife, Franny, lived across from

her place, Rebecca turned back to her
yard, the sign Noah had made for her a
few years ago now showing a fresh coat
of paint:

The Lily Lady.

The sign stated that in big black letters,
with a variety of painted daylilies underneath and an arrow pointing to her home
and the colorful fields beyond.

Ja, she was the lily lady all right. And
right now, she needed what the other sign
by her driveway asked for:

Help Wanted.

Dear Lord, send someone soon. Rebecca
was having a hard time finding a permanent handyman to help her with not only
the lilies but also everything else her parents' small farm required. Her helper of
the last few years, Moses Yoder, had decided to move to a community in Ohio to
be near his ailing sister. He'd left a month
ago and she still hadn't found anyone to
replace him.

Most men around here had to work their

own land or had a regular job. And the young folks didn't want to work in a hot field most of the summer. They found summer work elsewhere or had to help their own families get through the crops.

She looked toward the sky, expecting more dark clouds full of rain, but the sun shone brightly in the midmorning sky. What a wet week it had been. Hoping her bulbs wouldn't rot away instead of blooming, she made it back to the front porch and turned to see Katie waving to her from Noah's porch.

Rebecca waved back. Then she noticed something else.

A man walking along the road.

People walked by here all the time. Rebecca loved to walk and often did that since she didn't like horses.

But this man looked different.

When he turned toward her house, she gasped and went inside. She had a phone she used for business. She'd use it to call the police, too, if need be.

The man kept walking, his dark hair shaggy around his face, his jeans worn and tattered. He carried an aged olive-colored pack on his back. He wasn't Amish.

Rebecca watched from the kitchen window. He came up onto the porch and stood at the unlocked screen door. One knock. Then another.

"Hello, anyone home? I came about the help-wanted ad." He stopped and Rebecca heard a distinctive sigh. "I need a job."

Rebecca had hoped someone Amish would take the job. She needed a handyman who liked working with the earth, someone who understood the art of growing lilies.

This man didn't look like that type.

More like a beggar wanting a *gut* meal.

"Hello? I have references. Mr. Hartford from the general store showed me your ad," he called again.

References. She'd verify that. And Mr.

Hartford wouldn't send someone he didn't trust.

Yet, Rebecca hesitated. She wasn't sure what to do. She needed help now, and here he stood, asking for a job. She watched him turn, his shoulders hunched in dejection, his head down as he eased off the porch.

Her spring season was here. She needed someone, had just prayed about it, and so far, this was the only person who'd shown any real interest. Well, the only person who looked strong enough for what the work demanded. She'd turned down two scrawny teens because she knew them to be troublemakers, and a *grossdaddi* who only wanted to get out of his rocking chair. But he could barely get up the porch steps. No one else had even tried to apply.

What should she do?

Rebecca stilled for two heartbeats, then hurried to the door.

"Wait."

The man turned around and looked up

at her, his expression raw and edgy, dangerous. But his eyes—they held a world of hurt and pain. He looked broken. Completely broken.

She let out a little breath. He reminded her of someone—her deceased fiancé, John Kemp. Her heartbeat lifting to a new height, she blinked back tears. John had died when he was eighteen. Fifteen years ago. This stranger looked *Englisch*. He also looked lost.

"What's your name?" Rebecca asked, motioning him onto the porch while she gathered her composure. His features only reminded her of John, but then she thought every day of the man she'd loved and planned to marry. She had to be imagining things. No amount of longing could bring John back.

Jebediah," he said, his voice like splintered wood. "Jebediah Martin."

That name didn't ring a bell with her, so she tried to relax. Pointing him to a rocking chair, she sat down on a nearby bench. "And why do you need this job?"

He glanced out at the yard and then back to her. "Because I need work. I need... money. I've been traveling and I wound up here."

"You have references?"

"Yes, a couple from other jobs."

"Do you know anyone here?"

"No."

"How do I know I can trust you?"

"You don't know, but you can trust me. I need a job."

"What can you tell me that would make me trust you?"

"Nothing. You *can* trust me."

Rebecca tried again. "Do you like working outside, with flowers and gardens? Do you know how to plow—with a horse pulling the plows?"

"I know horses, but as for gardening, I've never done it before, but I can learn." He looked down at his old boots. "I know the earth, the seasons, the crops."

Rebecca lifted her hands, palms up, and let out an aggravated breath. "You're not impressing me."

The man finally looked directly into her eyes. "I told you I need a job. It's that simple."

Then he reached into the battered backpack and pulled out an envelope filled with folded papers. "Here."

He handed her two references—one from a restaurant owner in Indiana and one from a hotel where he'd cleaned rooms in Kentucky.

"These folks seem to think you're a *gut* worker."

"I am."

Trying hard to ignore the deep blue of his gaze, she said, "I grow lilies, you understand? I need someone with a strong back who can work long hours. I need someone to look after the horses—two of them. Red is the roan mare, and Silver is the draft horse. I have a small barn and stable. I have greenhouses and a vegetable garden and soon, my backyard and the lily field and the plant nursery will all be full of people buying lilies, other plants, and fresh vegetables. A lot of them *Englisch*."

"I can handle that."

"Horses?"

"I said I can handle horses. I grew up around horses."

She wondered if he could truly handle anything. With each question she asked, his eyes went dull and then lit up as if he'd just thought of that idea.

"What other jobs have you had besides the restaurant and cleaning hotels?"

He rubbed the dark stubble on his chin. "Let's see. Janitor. Bartender. Dog walker. Apartment cleaner. Trash man. Lumber company. Painter. Construction. Rented beach chairs to tourists in Florida."

Disbelief warred with curiosity. He'd been all around, it seemed. "But never gardening?"

"No. But... I like flowers. My mom used to grow a lot of flowers."

The way he said that coupled with the longing in his blue eyes told her what she needed to know. He was a black sheep, an outsider, a wayfarer. A man in need of something to cling to—in need of the earth and the wind, the sun and the rain. What should she do?

"Are you hungry?"

"Yes. And thirsty."

Rebecca made her decision, based on entertaining angels unaware. This man did not look like an angel, but he sure needed one. "Meet me around back and I'll bring you some lemonade and a sandwich. Do you like cookies?"

His eyes stayed bright on that question. "Yes."

Jeb walked around the neat, compact white farmhouse, noticing all the colorful flowers in the yard. This place was so pretty and prim, it almost hurt his eyes to take it all in.

But then, he'd seen the ugly side of life

for so long now, he'd forgotten that the earth was still beautiful.

He'd wound up here by sheer fate. Or God's will. After not finding work in another Pennsylvania community, Jeb had worked a few weeks with a building crew. But the whole operation got shut down due to outstanding permits. One night in his hotel room, he'd remembered some letters he'd kept through the years. Letters from his cousin who used to live here.

Campton Creek, Pennsylvania. He hopped on the next bus out and planned to find kinfolk here. Only, no one related to him still lived here. He'd gone into the local general store to buy some supplies, and while there he'd heard someone mention a local Amish woman was looking for help. Mr. Hartford had immediately told Jeb he should find out more.

The Lily Lady, they'd called her.

This little bit of earth was nice. This woman was nice, too, despite her many questions. Legitimate questions, but pushy, all the same. She had pretty freckles and sun-streaked dark blond hair covered with a white *kapp*—a prayer bonnet. That *kapp* reminded him of his *mamm*.

He was a long way from home, but this town had sounded so peaceful and serene in his cousin's letters.

This place—the Lily Lady's place—certainly brought that feeling to his soul. But he wasn't sure she'd hire him, and he wouldn't blame her if she didn't.

He came around the house and stopped to take it all in. Daylilies, rows and rows, some with hardy blossoms ready to pop open, some just about ready to grow and bloom. He could smell the mixtures of a thousand scents. Lilies of the field.

He did not want to leave.

"Here you go."

He turned to find her with a wooden tray full of food and a tall glass of lemonade, the condensation on the side of the glass shimmering like teardrops.

Jeb hurried to take the tray.

"*Denke*," she said, pointing to a table on the porch. "Sit and eat and I'll talk."

He smiled at that, his brain rattled at finding something to smile about. "Thank you for the food."

She nodded and tugged at a rebel strand of hair, tucking it behind her ear. "I live here alone, so I have plenty of leftovers."

After she said that, a wary glaze darkened her eyes. "My *bruder* and his family live across the road."

"So you're not too alone," he replied, hoping to reassure her. Then he decided to be honest. "I don't bite, and I'm not going to rob you or hurt you. As I said—"

"—you need a job," she interrupted, a soft smile on her face. "Let me see a few more reference letters."

Handing her the whole pack, he said, "Read whatever you want."

Jeb bit into the roast beef sandwich with fresh tomatoes. Then he took a swig of the freshly squeezed lemonade. "This is good," he said between mouthfuls.

She leafed through the references. "Don't forget the cookie."

He nodded and finished off the sandwich. "We can walk and talk if you'd like. I'll take the cookie with me."

"Bring your lemonade, too, then."

He got up and followed her. "This is all yours."

"Yes. I inherited it after my *mamm* passed on. We lost my *daed* five years ago, and Mamm and I lived here together until she had a heart attack two years ago. She loved helping me with the lilies."

"How did this come about?"

She laughed at that. "I love daylilies. I started planting ditch lilies, and then I planted more and learned how to cultivate them since they like to spread. At first, we gave them away but after Daed died, we needed money—an income— so we planted different varieties and put a sign on the road. People started coming to buy them. I added different varieties and learned which worked best. With my *bruder*'s help, we planted a small field and he put up the sign. And now, this is my life." She stopped and took a breath. "I'm known as the *alte maidal* lily lady."

"You are not old," he said. And regretted it when her eyes went wide.

"You can interpret *Deutsch*?"

He had to think quickly. "Only a few terms. I've worked with Amish on construction sites."

She didn't look convinced, but she nodded and started back walking. "The creek is back there." She pointed to the right. "We use irrigation from the creek on a limited basis."

"Pretty spot, there by the creek."

"Yes, it is." Her green eyes seemed to lose some of their shimmer. "You'd need to plow—that's where the horses come in. I don't like horses, so I usually have someone else handle them."

"I can do that. Me and Silver will get to know each other. And Red sounds like a nice lady."

"You'd also need to weed, fertilize with natural materials."

"You mean manure?"

"Ja." She laughed and it seemed the sun got brighter.

"I don't mind manure. Been in it a few times here and there."

She shook her head. "You do have a sense of humor."

"Yes." He rarely smiled this much in one day.

"We plant seedlings, we dig up bulbs and fans—the stems. We pamper the lilies, and we are open Monday to Thursday from nine to four. Friday is maintenance day. We open until noon on Saturday and never on Sunday."

"I don't mind the work," he said. "I like it here."

"You might change your mind during peak season when cars are parked all over the yard and children are running through the fields." She lifted her hand. "There are also the spring mud sales and festivals. I have a booth at all festivals, and we bring in a lot of income that way."

"I won't mind that either," he replied. "I'll do any work and I'll find solutions."

She stopped their stroll between the field and the barn. "Well, then, Jebediah Martin, I'm going to go on faith and trust you." She named his salary. "Is that fair?"

"More than fair," he replied, relief and gratitude moving through his frazzled system. "I can start Monday. I just need to find a place to live."

"I might be able to help with that, too," she said. "My *bruder* has an empty *grossdaddi haus*. He rents it out."

Surprised yet again, Jeb was beginning to think God had brought him to this place. "That might work."

"We can walk over to see him now if you'd like."

"Sure."

He put down his empty lemonade glass and hurried with her around the house.

"I'm sorry," he said. "I never got your name."

"Oh, that's my fault. You surprised me and I forgot. I'm Rebecca. Rebecca Eicher."

Jeb's heart dropped to his feet.

Rebecca.

Could this be possible? Was this the woman his cousin John Kemp had planned on marrying so long ago?

Chapter Two

There were a lot of women named Rebecca in the world, especially in an Amish community. He'd ask around to be sure, but while she chatted about rain and pests and pollen, he studied her with covert glances. Older, yes, but John had described a girl with dark blond hair and pretty green eyes.

This couldn't be possible, but the more he glanced at her, the more he became sure this was John's Rebecca.

Becca, John had said in his letters.

But John was no longer alive. Add to that, John and Jeb had kept their correspondence a secret, since Jeb's *daed* had been a Mennonite. His mother hadn't been shunned after she'd married Calvin Martin, but she'd faced an uphill battle between her faith and the man she loved. And so had her two sons. While she'd raised Jeb and his brother as Amish, Calvin Martin had made their lives hard on all accounts. The man might have grown up in a Mennonite home, but he'd had no scruples and no faith in God.

Jebediah had to sneak John's letters into the house, and he'd also had to be careful when replying with his own. While his *mamm* knew how close the cousins had become, she never mentioned the letters to her husband. But she sure enjoyed reading them in private after Jeb had read them, and she made sure it was his job to collect the mail. John's letters were the only way she got news from her sister, who sometimes tucked in her own messages.

Now here he stood, about to go to work for John's once-fiancée, Rebecca.

Should he ask her outright? No, not yet. He needed to work, to get his life back on track, to find himself and God again.

He couldn't hurt her by blurting out something that might *not* be true, or that *could* be true. Either way, he'd bring pain to her. She'd never married, obviously. The timing and her age added up, but he kept denying what he saw with his own eyes.

When they reached her brother's house, a little girl ran out onto the porch and giggled. "Aenti Becca, I got home all by myself. Why are you here?"

Becca.

The woman standing by him said, "I have a visitor. Tell your *daed* to please come out here."

A woman with dark hair appeared at the door. "Becca, so *gut* to see you. Did Katie forget to tell me something?"

Rebecca shook her head, while the other woman stared at Jeb, making him want to turn and walk away. "*Neh*, I need to talk to Noah about renting the *grossdaddi haus* to my new worker. Jebediah Martin, this is my sister-in-law, Franny."

Franny came out onto the porch. "I see." She kept her eyes on Jeb. "Nice to meet you."

He knew she didn't feel that way. The woman was petrified and curious about him being here. "Same here," he said, not knowing what else to do.

"Franny?" Rebecca's amused smile sprouted a dimple on her left cheek. "Where is Noah?"

"Oh, look at me not minding my manners. He's out back near the barn. Pulling weeds."

"I'll go and find him," Rebecca replied. *"Denke."*

Franny nodded. "Do you want something to drink?"

Jeb shook his head. At least he'd never go hungry here.

"Neh, but *denke,"* Rebecca said, motioning him around.

"Can I come?" the little girl named Katie asked.

Her mother grabbed her by the sleeve of her dress. "I need you in the kitchen with me."

Katie's bottom lip protruded in a pout, but she followed her mother all the same.

After they were around the corner of this bigger house, Rebecca whispered, "My *bruder* is the protective sort. He'll question my decision, but he will give in."

"If you say so," Jeb replied, thinking he should just walk away. He had no right to be here and if his guesses were true, his presence could bring pain to this kind woman. She might think he'd purposely come here to find her. He didn't know whether to let what he'd discovered stay unsaid, or just blurt out the truth.

Maybe if he got through the first week or so, then he could explain to her.

"There he is," she said, pointing to where a big man moved a hoe through some tall grass. "Noah?"

The man turned, his long beard holding a hint of gray, his straw hat low over his brow. "Sister, what brings you over? And who do you have with you?"

Rebecca walked closer to her brother. "This is Jebediah Martin, my new helper. I just hired him, and he needs a place to live while he's working for me."

Noah's brown-eyed gaze moved over Jeb like a hawk searching for a ground mole. "Is that right, now?"

"*Ja*, right as rain," Rebecca replied, her hands held together over her apron. "He needs a job and I need a helper."

Noah placed the hoe next to the barn. "And where are you from, Jebediah?"

Jeb had not thought about people knowing of him, but John had promised to keep their correspondence a secret to protect Jeb's mom. He'd be vague on the details, just in case. "Ohio."

"You have people here?"

"Not that I know of."

"But you are *Englisch*?"

"Yes." For now, anyway.

"He starts Monday," Rebecca went on. "Can he rent the *grossdaddi haus*?"

Noah's frown made him look like a hawk waiting for a mouse. "What do we know of this man, Becca?"

She shoved several of his references into her brother's hands. "He comes highly recommended."

Noah read over the short references. Jeb had been meticulous about getting references. They helped him find a lot of jobs. He hoped they'd work on this one.

"How do we know he didn't write these himself?"

Becca gave him a light shoulder tap. "Noah, these are handwritten, and some typed out. They have phone numbers to verify."

Jeb nodded. "They're real. I always ask for references before...before I move on."

"*Ja*, moving on. That concerns me," Noah replied. "Becca, you can't trust how long someone like this man will stay."

"I trust him for now," she said. "I need help. I prayed for help. He came walking up."

Noah handed the references back to her and dropped his hands to his side, eyeing Jeb with that intense frown again.

Jeb held his breath. If he lost this offer, he'd be at the end of the road. No hope left. He was tired of roaming.

Her brother glanced from Rebecca back to Jeb. "Could I have a word with my sister, alone?"

Rebecca stepped toward Noah. "I know what you're going to say. He's *Englisch*. He looks like a criminal. We don't know him. You don't want him hanging around me. Did I miss anything?"

Jeb held his lips tightly together to keep from laughing. But the serious look in Noah Eicher's eyes told him that would be a big mistake.

"That covers most of it," Noah said, his eyes on Jeb. "We can find someone within the community."

"I've tried that for a month now."

"Try harder. I don't like the looks of him."

Jeb held up his hand. "Whoa, I'm right here. I can see you don't want me here. But your sister and I talked all that out. I look this way because I don't have a home and I've been traveling around. But I work when I can find work, just to get back to the place where I need to be. Right now, this is the place I'd like to stay in for a while. I can do this work. I won't hurt your sister or do any damage to her property. I only want a good day's work for a good pay. She has offered me that."

Noah's dark expression softened. Then he shook his head. "You two should work well together. All that stubborn is burning a hole in the grass."

"Is that a yes?" Rebecca asked, her hands on her hips.

Her brother didn't seem so sure. "*Ja*, I reckon it is at that."

"*Gut*, because he's ready to move in on Monday."

Noah opened his mouth to speak, then shut it while he pondered this situation. "I'll have the place cleaned up and ready."

He named the rent price, and Jeb agreed.

Jeb extended his hand. "Thank you."

Noah took it, reluctantly, but held it in a firm warning of a grip. "Don't make me regret this."

Rebecca got up bright and early Monday morning and headed up the hallway toward the kitchen. After setting the kettle on for tea, she stood and looked out the kitchen window, marveling at the sunrise lifting out over the foothills and valleys. Her kitchen had windows on each side, front and back. Her *daed* had built it that way for her *mamm*.

"So you can see the day coming and see it ending," he'd told Mamm. Her mother had loved telling that sweet story.

Rebecca was sure glad he'd been so

thoughtful. Because while the sun did remain in one spot, the earth revolved around it, and her world revolved around her morning prayers by this window and her evening prayers at the one across the way by the old dining table and buffet. She was allowed the afterglow of dawn and dusk, almost every day, and the full sun on special days. This helped her remember the afterglow of her parents' abiding love. She might not ever have that, but she had her windows.

After she'd stood silent, her prayers a mixed bag of hope tempered with a lonely grief that never ended, she moved to the dining room and checked the fields. The buds just peeking out of the green field would open all the way in a few weeks. They'd bloom mostly from May through October, and some would keep blooming. The variations of her lilies, especially the hybrids, always amazed her. So much color, so much beauty. Some were more fragrant than others, but they were all perfect.

"*Denke*, Father."

She turned to make her tea and toast and brought her meal to the table. But something out the window caught her eye.

Jebediah Martin stood, dressed in Amish clothes, staring out over her lily field, his hands down by his side, his back to her.

Rebecca's breath caught in her throat and a swift piercing shot through her heart. She couldn't stop staring at the man she'd hired, but she wished with all her heart that her John was standing there, ready to start his day.

Before she could turn away, he pivoted and glanced toward the house, his gaze meeting hers. Rebecca stepped back from that intense glance. This man made her remember she was alone and lonely. She reminded herself that she had family to love, and she had a busy, blessed life.

Why should that change now?

She left the window and tried to eat her breakfast.

But she couldn't finish, so she took her

tea and walked out to where he waited. "Have you eaten?"

He nodded. "Yes. I found food on the counter when I got to the house. You have a kind family."

"We like to feed people. Let me finish up inside and I'll be out to get you started."

He nodded. "Mind if I go to the barn? I'd like to learn my way around."

"Go," she said, relieved that he'd found something to occupy him. Also relieved that she didn't have to give him a tour.

All weekend long, she'd wondered about hiring this man. She knew nothing about him, and he knew nothing about daylilies. They made a strange pair. The whole community would be gossiping, but Rebecca had learned to let gossip run its course. How was she supposed to do all this by herself? It was hard enough with someone helping her. She hired local youths during the summer months, but right now she needed a capable adult who didn't mind the work involved in preparing before her loyal customers came from all over to buy their lilies.

Did I do wrong?

She watched Jebediah go into the barn, her heart always escalating with fear when anyone got close to the horses. Sad, since she used to love the horses. But not now. Not after she'd witnessed John being thrown from an excited roan.

Thrown and killed.

Even though John's own horse had thrown him when a vehicle backfired on the road near his house, she had not been in the barn near her family's horses since then. Her brother and others kept up the stables for her. Relieved, she was glad this man didn't seem to mind dealing with that part of his job.

Rebecca turned toward the fields. She had two small ones, but between them, they yielded about two thousand rooted stems with fans per year. She'd try more if she had help.

Maybe this season.

Grabbing a hoe and basket, she hurried to the field, intent on getting rid of weeds before the day became warm. She loved late spring into early summer. The smell of lilies would wake her each morning and send her to sleep at the end of her day.

Lilies of the field, morning and night. She'd been content with that for so long.

But today, her contentment wasn't as serene as it had been last week, before he'd shown up. What an irony, that the Lord would send her someone to help, but that someone, that stranger, only reminded her of the life she'd lost the day she'd lost her John.

What kind of summer did she have ahead of her with this mystery man? She'd hired him on an impulse and out of a fear of failure. Those traits could do her in one day, but Rebecca remembered that *Gott*'s will would keep her steady. She also tried to convince herself that she didn't hire him on the spot because he resembled her deceased fiancé. That would make her truly pathetic.

She tore into her pruning and hoeing— sending weeds and trimmings flying into her basket, her mind recoiling from the longing in her heart.

Until a bronzed hand touched her aching shoulder. "Let me."

Jebediah knelt beside her at the end of a row.

She'd been so lost in her musings, she hadn't even noticed him or the time of day. "What?"

"It's noon and you've been at this all morning. Rest. I can finish these rows."

She stood, her hands automatically reaching for her tired back. "I'm sorry. I left you in the barn too long."

"It's okay. I introduced myself to the horses, put them out in the corral, cleaned the stalls and freshened the hay. I'll get back in there later at feeding time. I want to organize everything."

Rebecca glanced at the barn and then

back to him. "You've for certain sure been busy, ain't so?"

He gave her a direct gaze, his blue eyes battling with the sky. "I like staying busy."

She blinked, thinking too much sun had gone to her head. "*Denke*. I'll make dinner."

"Rest first. And, Rebecca, you don't have to feed me."

"Part of your pay," she said, glad to have someone *to* feed. Glancing around, she smiled. "Besides, I have a vegetable garden behind the barn. I'll need help with that, too. We get to eat the fruits of our labor."

"I like that idea. Do you have fruit trees, too?"

"Apples, blueberries, blackberries, cantaloupe late in the summer, pumpkins, turnips. I grow lots of vegetables. Beets—"

"I hate beets."

"I'll try to remember that," she said with a grin. "Do you like cranberries?"

"I do."

"I don't grow those."

"Too bad."

Rebecca motioned to him. "Before you finish what I started, *kumm* to the house and let's eat. I have cold chicken to make chicken salad. With sweet pickles and my secret ingredient."

"Not beets?" he asked, following her toward the house.

"No. Just a dash of paprika. Another sandwich on fresh sourdough. With chips."

"Chips?"

"I love potato chips," she said with a shrug.

"You are a woman full of surprises, Rebecca."

"We have that in common, then," she said on a saucy note. Maybe this would work out, after all. Jebediah seemed to like keeping to himself, same as her. But she hoped he'd open up about his own life and why he'd chosen to wander the earth, rather than plants roots in it.

Chapter Three

Day's end.

Jeb took a long breath. He'd sure enjoyed working again. He'd only been here a week, but this might be the best job he'd ever had—considering he got fed by everyone. He walked out of the barn and shut the big doors.

He'd taken care of the two horses. The roan, Red, was docile and sweet and the big draft, Silver, had a gray coat and white mane. Silver seemed spirited but dependable.

"Why don't you like horses?" he'd asked, curiosity getting the best of him.

Her pretty eyes had gone dark, a shutter falling across her smile. She'd glanced out at the barn. "They frighten me."

He'd left it at that, but he knew something bad happening usually caused people to fear animals. "I'll take care of them," he'd said. "You don't have to worry about that anymore. I've cleaned and rearranged all the bridles and harnesses and mended some of the reins that are worn. Saddles look good, but I polished them. And I washed the summer buggy and checked the wheels."

"You have been busy," she'd replied, a faraway look in her eyes. "I've neglected the barn for a long time."

Now, he turned away from the brilliant sunset that had become a mixture of clouds warring with color just over the tree line. Puffy gray had turned to muted yellows and pinks. The prettiest sunsets usually came with low-hanging clouds, because the clouds and clear, clean air reflected the sun in those brilliant hues.

He could spend the rest of his days here, watching the sun rise and set. This was a peaceful, beautiful place. But he'd only been here a few days. He and Becca were getting along. Each morning, she'd give him coffee and food if he hadn't eaten, then tell him what needed to be done. They worked together at times and alone at other times. She was a gentle boss. Things could change. He knew that.

Rebecca came down the back steps with a basket in her hand.

"What's that?" he asked, liking the easy way they could talk to each other.

"Your supper," she said with a soft smile. "Beef stew and potatoes with string beans. No beets."

He laughed. She made him laugh. "I have to remember that with the Amish, lunch is dinner, and dinner is supper."

"*Ja*, we like to eat, same as most."

"Now, I like to eat," he said. "But you don't have to feed me supper all the time. I can cook."

"Was that one of your jobs?"

"Yes, I've worked in a few restaurants and cafés." He shook his head. "I'm a wanderer."

"A wayfaring stranger?"

"Yes."

"Do you want to tell me a little about how you wound up here?"

"No. Not yet."

She looked away, as if she already knew she'd find him going up the lane to the road one day. "As long as I have you through the summer."

"I think I'll be here a good long while," he said, realizing that he meant it. "Especially for the meals."

She giggled. "Take your supper and go get cleaned up. You had a long first week."

"I liked my first week," he replied. "I'll see you tomorrow, early. More weeding?"

She nodded and lifted her arms. "Always weeding and pruning, sorting bulbs, planting bulbs and watering everything. But only a half day." Then she pointed to the basket she'd just handed him. "I know we've talked, and I've tried to explain everything to you, but I put some papers in there, about lilies and our schedule. That might help or you might leave in the middle of the night."

"I won't do that," he said. "Thank you."

She nodded and walked with him toward the front yard. "My *bruder*'s been busy with crops this week, but he will probably pay you a visit soon. He's protective." She waved her hand in the air. "I'm sure he managed to get in touch with some of those names on your reference papers."

"I'd expect that, having met him."

"He means well, but we have different mindsets regarding outsiders. He will worry that you and I work here alone together. But I think I'm far past needing a chaperone."

"And I was taught how to respect women."

She smiled at that, her eyes full of questions he wasn't ready to answer.

Jeb wanted to tell her he wasn't really an outsider. He'd left the Amish close to twenty years ago after a horrible accident and a disagreement with his rigid father, and he'd never dreamed he'd want to return. But would she understand and accept that, or that he was her John's long-lost cousin? He'd find the right time to tell her all of this, all about his life. But not yet. This would be a long summer, with plenty of daylight left to talk about the past.

They made it to the front and he turned to her. "I'll see you tomorrow, Rebecca."

"I'll be here, Jebediah."

"You can call me Jeb," he said, again not really thinking.

"Oh." Her eyes filled with shock and the darkness fell across her expression again. "Jeb. Only if you call me Becca."

"I can do that."

He turned, realizing his cousin John had called him Jeb. Had John mentioned that to her before?

Jeb Martin.

That nagging wonder she'd felt when this man first walked up the lane made

Rebecca stop and stare out toward the orange-tinged afterglow of the sunset. Why did he have to remind her of John? Why did Jeb seem so familiar to her?

You are imagining what you can't have.

She'd had men court her since John died, but she'd never gotten past a first outing or two. Telling herself she'd rather be alone, Rebecca had been so adamant on that, her friends and family had finally given up on trying to find her a husband.

Some frowned on her running a business on her own. But when she pointed out she was capable of taking care of herself, they usually quieted. She refused to live on handouts or the kindness of friends. She and her mother had made a nice enough living selling lilies. What was so wrong with her continuing to do that on her own?

This was what was wrong—this knowing she'd be alone for the rest of the day. With the sunlight, she had her work to keep her busy. But nighttime was lonely. She read by the propane lamp, mostly the

Bible, a few novels and bulb catalogs, *The Budget* newspaper, and other weekly papers.

Boring. She had a boring, but peaceful existence. Now that existence had been shifted and rearranged by this man showing up out of the blue to ask for work.

Shaking her head, Rebecca went about getting her supper on a plate. She glanced at the calendar she kept on a small desk in the living room and saw that tomorrow, her sister, Hannah, was coming by to help with canning some early vegetables. They always had fun together with their Saturday frolics. Hannah was younger and newly married to Samuel.

That usually didn't bother Rebecca, but all the longing she'd managed to hide so well for the past fifteen years came back full force. She'd never be married. She'd missed her time for marriage and a family. *Gott's will.*

She shouldn't question the Lord's plans for her, but today she'd certainly been near to doing that. She took her plate out onto the back porch to enjoy the last of dusk while she nibbled at the food. At least she had someone who seemed capable to help her through the summer. Would Jebediah—Jeb—decide to stay longer?

Did she want that?

You don't know this man.

No, she didn't know him. But she felt she should know him. He'd done all the work she'd heaped on him and done it without complaint. They worked together, but he left her alone once she issued him a task. She'd had a few early customers this week and he'd stayed in the background, absorbing and learning, then offering to load up the purchased plants.

He learned quickly and seemed to be well educated.

He'd made it clear he might wander off again. She needed to remember that and maybe start looking for a permanent solution while he was still available. Surely someone in the small community of Campton Creek needed a steady job.

She wanted to ask him more about what had made him become a nomad, a wanderer, a loner. But that was none of her business.

She'd ask around in a discreet manner. Well, as small communities went, she'd try.

She wondered if people passed on her job offer because no one wanted to work with the old maid lily lady. Why did marriage have to define a woman's status? She knew her faith demanded certain things and she understood that but being alone wasn't much fun at the end of the day. Was it prideful to want to be strong and self-sufficient so she wouldn't need to rely on the kindness of others?

The food tasted *gut*, but like most things, food was better when shared with company. Rebecca thought about the few meals she'd had with Jeb. He made her laugh and challenged her with his worldly talk and all the occupations he'd tried.

She needed to know why he liked to roam around. She wanted to understand why he made her think of John.

She set her plate down and put her hands in her lap, her unfinished food on the table beside her, her head down in silent prayers.

Then she heard a voice. "Rebecca?"

Looking up, she saw Jeb standing there. Startled, she stood. "What is it?"

"Nothing," he said, his hair clean and combed back off his face, a new shirt smelling of her sister-in-law's detergent. "I… I need a haircut and… I thought maybe you could help me with that?" Shrugging, he went on. "I meant to ask earlier and well, I forgot."

Rebecca bobbed her head, while her heart came to a skidding halt. The man needed a haircut, so why was she being a ninny. "I have scissors. We can set a chair in the grass, and I'll give you a trim."

"I'd appreciate that," he said. "Will you be able to see?"

"I think we have a few minutes before full dark," she replied. "If not—we'll see how I do when daylight returns tomorrow."

He grinned. "Okay, then."

Rebecca rushed inside to get a towel and her scissors.

She prayed her shaking hands didn't give Jeb the worst haircut ever.

Jeb sat in the high-backed chair and waited. He should have put this off until later, but after he'd cleaned up for the day, he realized his hair was too shaggy. Since he had no way into town to find a barber, he'd thought of Rebecca.

Dumb idea.

Now the pretty woman who was his boss would be running her hands through his hair. At least it was clean and smelled like some sort of flower garden, thanks to the goat's milk soap Franny had left for him by the kitchen sink in his tiny house.

Rebecca came back out of her house with a towel and scissors. "Do you want me to take off a lot or a little?"

He grinned. "I don't want a shaved head. Maybe just an inch or so and trim my bangs."

"I promise I won't put a bowl over your head," she teased, her laughter like wind chimes in his head. "Sit up straight and don't move."

"Yes, ma'am."

She shook her head at that, then started combing his hair. "You have a lot of hair."

"I know. Do you see that little bit of gray?"

"I think we all have that."

He thought about her hair and wondered how pretty it would look if she could wear it down. Which was forbidden, of course. Only her husband could see that. And obviously, she didn't have a husband.

As a teenager, he'd chafed under the

Amish tenets, but after some of the things he'd witnessed through the years out there in the world, he didn't find it so bad now. Maybe, like his strict *daed* had suggested he should do long ago, he'd finally become a mature adult.

"Okay, here I go."

He felt her hands on his neck, a little jolt of awareness going down his spine. Jeb blinked and refocused, his eyes on the rows and rows of green lily leaves across from them. He'd read over her reports while he'd enjoyed the home-cooked meal she'd given him. Growing lilies required nature's blessings and a human's hard work. But he thought it might be the best work for him, since he could gather his thoughts and process what he wanted to do next, while he gathered lilies and pulled up weeds. His mother used to say God was in all gardens.

He prayed God would touch his heart in this garden and show him the way when he reached the end of the row.

Rebecca's nearness brought him back to the gloaming. The sun shimmered over the trees, hovering in regret, not wanting to slip away. The air was soft and silent, as if a lightweight blanket had come down to comfort the world. Peace. He felt an intense peace sitting here.

Rebecca snipped and brushed his damp hair while he tried to ignore the feeling of her fingers against his skin, her touch as soft and quiet as the very air they were breathing. Maybe this had been a bad idea, after all.

She came around front. "Now your bangs. They like to curl, *ja*?"

"Uh-huh." He pretended to be looking out beyond her, but she was so close he could smell lavender and a hint of jasmine.

More of that homemade soap, he figured.

She'd just finished trimming his bangs, her comb flying through his new cut, when someone came stomping across the yard.

"Becca, what do you think you're doing?"

Her brother Noah came charging toward them, a mad rage in his dark eyes. "This is not acceptable behavior. You need to stop right this minute."

Becca stood back, her eyes going wide. "Noah, calm down. He needed a haircut."

"He could have let me do that," Noah said, his hands on his hips. "You know this is not right."

"I'm all done," Rebecca replied, her blush showing even in the waning light. "And I dare say, I think I've done better than you would have."

"I don't like this at all," Noah said. "I'm going to ask around to find you more suitable help."

"Neh," she replied, her scissors clutched in one hand. "I have hired someone, and Jeb has proved he's capable of taking care of things for me."

"He might be capable of a lot more," Noah said, his words thrown out like rocks. "And that will not go over well with me, and probably not with the bishop."

Jeb stood and moved away from Rebecca. "It's my fault. I asked her to trim my hair. I didn't think it would cause any trouble."

"You are trouble," Noah said. "I don't like this."

Rebecca moved to stand between Jeb and her brother. "Noah, do you think I'd do anything to dishonor myself or you, or anyone who knows us? I certainly won't stray from our ways. Jeb knows that. I was only cutting his hair and no harm came to anyone. I didn't even nick his skin."

"I'm not worried about his skin," Noah replied, his tone firm. "You mark my word, no good will come of this."

Jeb held up a hand. He had to stop this, or he'd be out of a job. But he wouldn't let Rebecca's brother make her feel bad on his account.

"Understood," he replied to Noah's heated words. Then he turned to her. "Rebecca, thank you. Noah, I get that you don't trust me but there's something you both need to know about me. Something that might help in relieving your concerns."

"What's that?" Noah asked, his eyes still blazing with distrust.

Rebecca shot Jeb a confused glance. "What is it, Jeb?"

Jeb took a deep breath and prayed he was doing the right thing. "I...know your ways, I know all the rules, I have read the *Ordnung*. I used to be Amish."

Chapter Four

Rebecca couldn't speak. All the signs were there, but she'd somehow ignored or missed them. He could understand some *Deutsch*, he knew his way around a barn and a farm, and he was humble and worked hard. Could those traits and mannerisms be the reason he reminded her of John?

She cleared her throat and looked at Jeb. "Why didn't you tell me that sooner?"

Noah held his hands on his hips. "*Ja*, that would have been a *gut* starting point."

Jeb sank down on the porch steps. "I've been away from the Amish for twenty years. I left my community in Ohio during my *Rumspringa*." He shrugged. "My *daed* and I didn't see eye to eye on anything. I left after we had an argument, and I never went back." He wouldn't tell them the rest now. They'd probably ask him to leave if he became completely honest.

Noah's anger moved from boiling to a simmer. "Why did you come here? Why not go back to Ohio?"

"I have no one in Ohio," Jeb said, his eyes dark, a forlorn expression on his face. "My *mamm* passed when I was a teenager, and I lost my only brother. He was thirteen when he died."

"Oh, Jeb, I'm so sorry." Rebecca knew his pain, had seen it in his eyes. It reflected her own torment. "That must have been so hard on your parents and you."

"It was, for me and my dad. My mom had passed already." He stopped and shook his head. "After Pauly died, things got worse between my dad and me. So... I left. I regret that now. Leaving my *daed* alone like that—it was wrong."

"You could still go to him," Noah suggested, his tone full of understanding. "My *daed* and I had fights, but we forgave each other. That is the Amish way."

"I tried that," Jeb said. "He became ill about five years ago, but he died before I could get home. The farm went into foreclosure and was sold at auction. I have no home now."

This explained some of his sadness and why he roamed around so much. He must blame himself terribly for losing his father and the farm, and after he'd lost his mother and brother, too. What a heavy burden for a person to carry.

"*Ja*, you do have a home," Rebecca said. "You have a home here in Campton Creek. We will make sure of that, won't we, *bruder*?"

Noah looked doubtful. "Do you want to return to the Amish for *gut*?"

Jeb nodded. "That is why I came here."

"Why here?" Noah asked, still being stubborn.

Jeb sat silent for a moment, then pushed at his new haircut. "I've been all over this country and a...friend told me about Campton Creek and the small community here. I don't know why I came, but I'm glad I found my way to this place."

He glanced at Rebecca, his gaze moving over her with renewed hope. "I like the work, and I can be good at it once I learn what I need to know."

Noah grunted. "We still have to consider you working here with Becca, day in and day out. Staying at my place means when the day's work is done, you do not return to visit my sister."

Rebecca tried not to roll her eyes. "Noah, I don't turn away visitors. And I don't mind feeding someone who works hard all day. Or cutting their hair."

Noah huffed and nodded. "Then it's settled. I'll be sending Adam over to work for you—as long as needed. That is the only way I'll agree to Jeb's staying. Adam and he will return to my side of the road at sunset every day, or I'll *kumm* checking."

Rebecca wanted to stomp her foot in frustration. "You need the boys to help you."

"I can spare one. Adam is the youngest at twelve. But he has *gut* eyes and *gut* ears. He will report back to me."

"I will not have you forcing your son to spy on me," Rebecca said, her hands now on her hips.

Jeb stood and held up both hands as if to separate them. "Enough. Noah, I've tried to tell you I will not dishonor your sister or my job. She would fire me on the spot if I tried anything *dumm*. Since I like this job and want to work, I will not be stupid. Either you accept that now, or *I* will have to walk away."

Rebecca gave him an imploring glance. "I haven't fired you, Jeb. You can't leave in the middle of my busiest season. Noah has no say on that regard."

Noah glanced from Jeb to Rebecca. "I should make you do just that. But Rebecca is of her own mind on these matters. Probably why no man will come near her."

Rebecca let out a shocked gasp, then whirled and headed for the house. "So, what are you fussing about? No man wants me, ain't so. I should be completely safe with Jeb."

She grabbed up her unfinished meal and held her scissors up with her free hand. "I'm surprised Jeb hasn't already left."

Then she went inside, the door slamming on her discontent.

Noah gave Jeb a long stare. "Well, that went as expected. She is easy to anger sometimes. Most times."

"You hurt her feelings," Jeb replied, angry on Becca's behalf. "You should know not to speak like that to a woman."

"I should, but I guess I'll never learn," Noah said. "Women have unpredictable ways, and I don't need unsolicited advice from a stranger. You're the reason she's angry."

Jeb bristled. "I'm not the one who made a rude remark about her. We've been getting along fine." He shook his head. "Go ahead and tell me I'm fired. See how she reacts to that."

Shrugging, Noah glanced toward the house. "You don't need to quit. She does need someone, and you seem willing to return to the brethren." Then he reached out his hand to Jeb. "I'm still sending Adam over to help out."

Jeb shook Noah's hand, silent. He worried about Rebecca more than he worried that Noah would send him packing. "I don't mind having a youngie to help out here and there, and Rebecca will be glad for it, too, I'm thinking."

Noah let go of his hand and smiled, surprising Jeb. "I'm beginning to think this situation will take care of itself. If you mean to stay here, you'll need to see the bishop and brush up on our ways. You'll

have to go before the church and ask forgiveness." Then he leaned in. "And you
will surely have to follow our tenets. If
you show me how badly you want that," he
said, glancing toward the house, "I might
begin to believe you could be one of us.
And that it will do my sister some *gut* to
have a strong, purposeful man around."

Jeb got the message, but he would not
be bossing Rebecca around. She seemed
to have her confidence under control. "I'll
show you more than that. I'll work hard on
all fronts. This is the most beautiful spot
I've seen in a long time."

He didn't tell Noah, but he also thought
Rebecca was the most beautiful woman
he'd seen in a long time.

But Jeb would keep that particular ob-
servance to himself.

Rebecca hadn't slept well. Finding out
Jeb was Amish had been both a blessing
and a shock. While she celebrated his return to the fold, she had to wonder why

he'd withheld that from her when she'd hired him.

After she slammed into the house, he and Noah had walked home. She'd watched them out the window, her mind reeling with all that Jeb had told her. He'd never opened up before, so she knew his admission had been hard on him. He'd been forced, since her brother wouldn't stop pestering them.

Jeb had confessed as a last resort so he wouldn't be fired, but if he'd been honest up front, she would not have held that against him. Maybe the shame of being away so long had kept him from explaining. Or was there more to his story?

Her brother had taken the news much better than Rebecca, but as was the case with Noah, he had stipulations. She knew Adam needed work to keep the boy calm but sending him to her seemed like a punishment and a shout of mistrust from her well-meaning brother.

After finishing the cup of tea she'd made

to eat with the slice of apple pie she'd decided to have for breakfast, Rebecca gathered her garden tools and headed to the herb bed she'd started in a raised box near the back door. She loved cooking with fresh herbs, so she'd planted basil, oregano, mint and parsley, along with rosemary, dill and thyme, and a few sweet peppers. Sometimes, she'd take a bit of bread dough and make her own pizza, covered with her own fresh sauce, goat cheese, vegetables, and herbs. Her treat to herself.

She wondered if Jeb liked pizza.

Why did that matter? Her brother would make sure he was fed at the house, just to keep Jeb from hanging around to have supper with her after the workday had ended. Noah's words to her last night still hurt. Why did people judge her for not having a husband? And why would they judge her for finding a strong, hardworking man to help her?

It didn't matter. She'd have to stay professional with Jeb, so her brother would stop having tantrums about her being alone with a man. Now that Jeb had admitted he was once Amish, maybe Noah would back off a bit. Or that could make matters worse.

Her mind whirling with that predicament, Rebecca didn't hear Jeb approaching until he was right up on her.

"Oh," she said, putting a hand to her chest. "You scared the daylight out of me."

He backed away, a frown darkening his face. "I didn't mean to startle you. Just reporting for work."

"Grumpy this morning?" she asked as she put down her trowel and took off her gardening gloves. "My brother does that to people."

Jeb's smile held a bit of understanding. "He's only trying to protect you. And you did warn me about that."

Rebecca crossed her hands over her stomach. "Jeb, why didn't you tell me right away?"

He looked down at his brogans. "I wanted to say a lot of things to you, but I wasn't sure how to go about it. I decided if you gave me this work, I'd keep quiet and do my job. And I hoped I could ease my way into my past."

"I don't think that worked for you," she replied, turning back to the tiny buds of green covering the foot-square sections of the long garden box. "Honesty is important in any relationship. We work together, so if there is anything else that I need to know about you, tell me now. I want the truth. That's all I ask of you."

Jeb couldn't look at her. He wanted to explain everything, but he'd jumped one hurdle by telling Becca and her overbearing brother that he was Amish. Or had been Amish at one time.

Did he really want to do this? Return to this world and make a life for himself here among strangers?

So far, the answer was yes, but the confrontation last night only reminded him of all he was hiding. Not just that he was related to Rebecca's beloved John, but all the secrets Jeb held closely to his heart. Would she want him to stay if she knew everything about him?

He couldn't risk that, not yet.

He lifted his gaze to Becca. "I have nothing much left to reveal. I have no money, no family, and no future unless I start right here and now. I want to make enough money to get me started, then I hope to find a place of my own."

He wanted to add that he could be happy working here the rest of his days, but that would only make things worse at this point. He'd work the summer and then leave. She'd never need to know he was related to the man she'd loved and lost. "I don't want to jeopardize my job, Becca."

"Your job is safe," she said after a moment of eyeing him. "I'll handle my *bruder* and his concerns."

"I think he'll be better now," Jeb said.

"We had a good talk when we walked home together. I think he now regrets what he said to you."

"That's fine," she said. "He was so kind to point out that I'm blessed to have you, since I'm such a bitter old maid."

"You are not old," he reminded her. "We're practically the same age."

She gave him a confused, questioning glance, as if she wanted to ask him more questions. Then she looked out over the lily field. "Some days, I feel old," she admitted. "My brother has a point. I've missed my prime. He knows I'm bitter. I was about to be married, long ago. But one horrible accident ended that."

Jeb wanted to take her in his arms and tell her to stop listening to her brother. Instead, he grabbed a hand tiller and started helping her weed the herb box. "You are only as old as you feel inside," he told her. "Let's pretend we're young again. It's a pretty spring day and we have the afternoon off. I'd like to go fishing."

She looked up at him, then glanced out toward the creek. "I have poles and you'll have to dig for bait but do whatever you wish."

"I was hoping you'd come with me."

Rebecca pushed at her *kapp*. "Oh, I have things to do. All day."

Disappointed, Jeb thought it was for the best. Noah wouldn't like seeing them fishing together. "Okay. I'm sure I'll catch the biggest fish you could imagine and then you'll be sorry you missed it."

"You can brag about it all you want," she retorted, her tone firm. "But I can cook whatever you catch. Hope you like frog legs."

"Oh, you think I'll only catch frogs?"

"I don't know yet, but maybe."

They both worked their way around the long rectangular garden box, clearing weeds and pruning heavy plants so the herbs could grow better. The scents of the tiny buds and unfurling greenery made Jeb think of home cooking and Sunday dinners. He'd had a lot of meals in greasy-spoon diners and fast-food places, so all the fresh, organic food here tasted even better than he remembered from his *mamm*'s cooking.

"I can't wait to use some of these," Becca said. "I'll sneak you meals when my brother isn't looking."

"That's a great idea."

Jeb went to grab a trowel at the same time she leaned over to get the watering jar.

They bumped heads.

"Ouch," she said, lifting up to rub her forehead.

He held her arm with one hand and his head with the other. "We both have hard heads. That hit me on my temple."

"*Ja.*" She started laughing, her eyes prettier than the green grass and trees. "I've been called hardheaded at times."

"Me, too."

Jeb laughed with her, his hand still on

her arm. Giving her a careful once-over, he asked, "Are you okay?"

Becca nodded. "I think we'll both have a knot."

He leaned close, studying her forehead. "Red right now."

She did the same with him. "Yours, too."

Then their eyes met, and Jeb's heart stilled for a moment.

Becca's eyes widened, a soft gasp escaping her mouth.

A current sizzled like a sweet longing in the air between them. He'd never felt anything like it, and he didn't want this moment to end.

Then a female voice called out, "Sister, what are you doing?"

Becca whirled so quickly, she almost hit Jeb again.

"Hannah, I thought you weren't coming until later."

"It is later," the woman said with a wide grin. "And not a minute too soon, from the look of things."

Chapter Five

"So this is the hired help," Hannah said with a grin while she watched Rebecca run around the kitchen to fix their noonday meal. "I had heard a lot about him already. Noah is fussing and stomping like an old bull."

Rebecca shoved a glass of iced tea toward where Hannah sat in a high-backed chair at the dining table. She'd planned to feed Jeb, too, but he'd taken off to his place to "eat a sandwich."

"Noah stomps around fussing about everything I do," she retorted. "Does he pester you about your choices and your household?"

Hannah nibbled on a sliced carrot. "*Neh*, but I'm married. I have a husband to do that."

Rebecca let out a sigh as she sliced cold chicken to go with the potato salad she'd made last night. "So that's the reason Noah watches me like a hawk?"

"I think so," Hannah said, her hazel eyes wide with understanding. "He means well, but he worries."

"I'm fine," Rebecca said, "but he upset me last night. Jeb asked me to cut his hair and I did so, out in the backyard. You'd think I was walking out with him without a chaperone or something." She told Hannah what Noah had said. "He's never talked like that to me before."

Hannah waited for Rebecca to join her for their light meal. "Sister, we both worry about you. I know you're independent and capable, but don't you want someone in your life?"

Rebecca looked at her plate. "Of course, I'd like that. But I haven't found that someone. I fear I might not ever find anyone, and I have to be okay with that. I have family. You and Noah, Franny and the *kinder*, and our community. I love my work here. I'm content."

"Content is one thing," Hannah replied. "Being happy is another."

"I was happy once," Rebecca said. "I'm as happy as I can be these days."

"Jeb makes you smile," Hannah said before she scooped up a spoonful of chicken salad and chewed, her eyes bright with mischief.

"We get along," Rebecca replied, shocked at her sister's antics. "He works hard and he's easy to be around."

"And not bad on the eye."

"You are a married woman," Rebecca admonished. "Don't let Andrew hear you talking like that."

"You know I love Andy. But I wish the same for you."

Rebecca ate some of the potato salad. "Are you suggesting Jeb would be a *gut* match?"

"From what Noah told me this morning, he was once Amish," her sister replied. "He could be again with a little coaching."

"So, you're suggesting that I coach Jeb into becoming Amish and then becoming my husband?"

"I might be…"

Rebecca put down her fork. "Did Noah put you up to this? Did he hurry to your house early this morning to ask your help in planning out my life for me?"

"You're angry," Hannah said.

"You haven't answered my question."

"He might have mentioned that Jeb seems to be a *gut*, strong man. And that there's really only one tiny problem."

"Jeb is not Amish anymore."

"Yes, that is the concern, but he has indicated he'd like to come home to his roots, to become one of us again. You could help in that area."

Rebecca shook her head and laid her hands on the table to keep her temper from erupting. "Let me get this straight. The *bruder* who fussed at me and told me no man would want me anyway has decided that the very man he's so worried about being around me is now the perfect man to be my husband?"

Hannah bobbed her head. "*Ja*, that sums things up. What do you think?"

"I think you are both *lecherich*."

"I'm not being ridiculous, Becca," Hannah replied. "This could be a *gut* solution for both you and Jeb."

Matchmaking seemed to be the pastime around here, especially when a new man came to town. Was she that pathetic?

"Not if Jeb and I don't want it." Rebecca gave up on finishing her meal. "I can't believe you let Noah talk you into such a foolish task. Jeb has been here a little over a week and has just now admitted what he hopes for his future, and you two already have our lives planned."

"Noah feels better knowing Jeb wants to make amends and come back to the Amish way of life."

"*Ja*, I'm sure he does. He's found a man to pass off his lonely, bitter sister to." She wanted to scream, but she refused to upset her sister. Hannah had been a pawn in Noah's persuasive hands. "I will discuss this with my *bruder* as soon as I see him again. If I ever speak to him again."

"You don't mean that." Hannah shook her head. "He lives right across the way. That would be hard to do since you see him almost every day."

"I can avoid him, but you are right. That would be hard to do since I love Franny and the *kinder*."

"You love Noah, too," Hannah said, giving Rebecca a wry smile. "He loves us even when he oversteps. Remember how he followed Andrew around, telling him exactly what he could and could not do around me?"

Rebecca had to laugh at those memories. "He didn't want Andrew to even look at you or hold your hand. Makes courting a bit difficult, ain't so?"

Hannah giggled. "Imagine if you and Jeb were truly serious about courting. Noah would sit between you in every buggy ride."

They started laughing, both of them wiping at their eyes.

When they heard a knock at the back screen door, Hannah actually snorted. "Probably Noah wanting to know when the wedding is."

Jeb stood there, staring at them with an inquisitive glance. Rebecca looked up and saw him, her laughter ending as she poked her sister.

"Jeb, *kumm* in," she managed to sputter.

He looked so distraught, she feared something had happened.

"Are you planning on getting married?" he asked, glancing from her to her sister.

Hannah burst out laughing again.

While Rebecca blushed, her face going hot.

"Not anytime soon," she replied. Then

she gave her sister a warning glance. "My sister was telling me a bad joke, that's all."

Jeb looked confused and maybe a little curious. Or she could be imagining things since her sister had planted that seed in her head. Jeb wasn't ready for marriage. First, he needed to find himself again and return to his faith. That could take a while. And second, she was in no hurry to marry just to please her siblings and this community.

But Hannah still had a big smile on her face.

Jeb had never understood women. Laughing one minute, in tears the next. They scared him with all the drama and emotions. His own *mamm* had been kind and quiet, following his *daed*'s every word or order. For a long time Jeb thought all women acted that way, but when he realized his mother was not happy, but just pretended to be, his heart hurt for her. His *daed* had not been a kind man. Not even before his brother, Paul, had died. Even more so after.

After his *mamm* passed away, Jeb tried to so hard to take care of Paul. Pauly, as they nicknamed him, had some issues. Slow, his *daed* called the boy. Mamm always said Pauly was a true blessing from *Gott*. After she passed from a rare disease, Pauly got even worse with tantrums and outbursts. Daed didn't like that. Then as Pauly grew older, things escalated. Jeb had to work to keep his family together. Pauly would run away and show up at Jeb's workplace, a buggy repair shop down the road.

Then one day he came to the shop and Jeb had been busy. He was harsh to his brother and Pauly ran toward home... didn't show up. Pauly didn't come back home. He'd been hit by a vehicle—ran right out in front of it. The driver kept telling everyone that the kid just came running across the road.

Jeb stopped remembering. He couldn't

go back and change things. His family was gone. With God now.

But he could work on the weeds in the yard, and he could get a head start on pruning the lilies. Rebecca had told him they'd start potting the healthier plants to sell on the road and at festivals.

He'd gulped down a thrown-together sandwich with some tea for his noon meal. Now he hoped the sisters were over whatever they'd been discussing earlier. He couldn't figure why the thought of Rebecca possibly being engaged had taken him so by surprise. She would have mentioned that to him. But then, they'd been wary of each other from the beginning, and he still held his secrets close. Why would he expect her to share the details of her life?

Maybe they *had* been telling a bad joke and he'd come in on the punch line. He'd see how Rebecca acted when her sister left.

He only had to work till noon, but he'd

stayed to get some things done and he had to check on the animals anyway.

And maybe, just maybe, he wanted to see how Rebecca was doing since they'd bumped heads. Then he smiled.

Probably wouldn't be the last time that happened.

Rebecca waved to her sister, then turned to head to the back of the house. With an afternoon off from work, she felt at odds. She had some mending to do, and she'd promised Katie a new summer dress for church. She and Hannah had cut out the pattern and she'd sew the dress together. That task could wait. She'd walk the perimeters of the lily field and see if anything needed her attention. The next few weeks would become busy. Locals and tourists alike would show up for lilies. Some wanted several to plant beds in their gardens. Others just wanted one to put in a pot or a special corner. She loved seeing people smile when they found the perfect hybrid. She had a special garden for shows, as many of her returning customers liked to display their plants in the local garden shows.

When she reached the back porch, she stretched and glanced around the property. Then she saw Jeb down at the creek with a fishing pole. He had invited her to go with him earlier, but she'd declined.

Should she at least walk down there now? Would that only add fuel to her brother's wishes for her?

Deciding to defy Noah and just be a friend to Jeb, Rebecca grabbed two glasses of lemonade and two oatmeal cookies from the batch she and Hannah had baked, and slowly made her way to where he stood by the bench she'd had the local furniture maker, Tobias Mast, build for her. She loved to watch the sunset from there. The wooden bench had a lily carved on the high back.

Maybe Noah wouldn't come running

around the house, demanding a wedding, if she sat on the bench while Jeb fished.

"Hello," she called as she neared where he stood near a short pier. "I thought you might be thirsty."

He held his pole but turned to smile at her. "I am at that. I did some weeding and walked the field. I like walking through the lilies." He glanced back at the grid of rows, all with a different variety of lily. "I'm learning to identify the names, based on the charts you gave me. Some are really fragrant, and others hold a faint scent. *Hemerocallis*, day beauty. That's the technical name from the Greek." Then he added, "But daylilies are different from lilies, right? They got that name because they only bloom for a day or so."

"You have been studying," she said, impressed. "And yes, you are correct. Most lilies started in Asia, but the *Englisch* especially loved them—the Eng*lish* in England that is. America got a late start, but now they are highly popular. Obviously, or I wouldn't be in business." She glanced back at the field. "That's why I have two fields. One is purely daylilies, and the other is more exotic lilies that need pampering and watching closely. I've come up with some unusual hybrids."

"I hope I can learn all the varieties," he said. "We could do hybrids this summer—come up with our own lily."

"What would we call it?" she asked, her heart thumping against her apron. Their own lily?

"The JeBecca," he teased.

"Or the Beccediah," she shot back.

"Or just the Becca," he replied, his tone soft and low.

"I never thought of naming one after myself."

"I'll name it—that way I get all the credit."

She pushed at his shoulder, noting how firm his muscles were. Quickly pulling back her hand, she grinned at him. "We'll see about that."

"But we can call them *Tetraploids*, too." He laughed. "It's confusing when they are really just beautiful flowers."

Rebecca nodded in agreement, gathering her scattered emotions. "You didn't have to work overtime."

"I didn't mind. You needed the time with your sister."

"I did," she admitted, trying to put what he'd suggested out of her head. Hybrids with their names joined. A wild suggestion. Naming a lily after her, even more so. Getting back to earth, she said, "Normally, Hannah comes by on Saturdays since I sometimes get last-minute guests who can't wait to buy lilies. She helps me with the money and such."

"She seems like a nice girl."

"*Ja*, wait until you get to know her. *Mischief* is her middle name." Rebecca laughed again. "She's married to Samuel Yoder. He's related to Moses Yoder, the man who used to work here."

Jeb nodded at that. "She surely had you laughing this morning."

How much had he heard? Rebecca didn't dare tell him what they'd discussed. Noah sending Hannah to push Rebecca onto Jeb. It was *baremlich*—terrible.

"We like to tease each other, and we compare notes on our overbearing brother. She's married now, so I'm the one he finds fault with most. I'm surprised he hasn't *kumm* running to fuss at us for fishing."

"Noah?" Jeb grinned. "I saw him leaving with his family a little while ago. I reckon they have plans for the day."

She wanted to say that was *gut* to hear. Instead, she replied, "They go to the Hartford General Store to buy supplies. It's a perfect day for a buggy ride."

"A perfect day for fishing, too," he said. "I've caught two nice bream and I have a frying pan waiting for them."

She sat on the bench and offered him a glass of lemonade. "Sounds like a *gut* supper to me. You can take some tomatoes to add. Do you have potatoes?"

He put down his pole and took the lemonade and a cookie. "I don't have any potatoes. I could stir-fry them and slice the tomatoes."

"I'll gather them when you're finished fishing."

"Denke." He glimpsed back toward the house and then looked at her. "May I sit here with you for a moment or two?"

She nodded. "Longer than that, Jeb, if you'd like."

He slid onto the bench, leaving a measure of space between them. "So if you were engaged, you'd have mentioned that, right?"

She decided to tease him a bit. *"Ja,* in the same way you mentioned you were once Amish." Then she smiled. "Gotcha."

Jeb shook his head and bit into his cookie. "I can see your sister is not the only one who has mischief on her mind."

Rebecca laughed and ate her cookie.

"You'd better keep an eye on your pole. I've heard there is a big bass roaming this creek."

"He might already be in my fishing net, floating just beneath the surface."

"Ah, so you can make jokes, too."

"Every now and then," he admitted.

She laughed and wished this kind of day could last forever. The buzz of bees, the wind singing through the trees, the scents of spring. For the first time in a long time, Rebecca felt hope in her heart.

Then she looked into Jeb's eyes and saw John there.

John should be here on her bench, not a stranger who was lost like a prodigal. Jeb was a kind person, and a handsome man. But could anyone ever measure up to her John?

Her laughter died down and she looked out over the water, no words forming on her lips. Tears formed in her eyes while she remembered how happy she'd once

been. Why did this man have to remind
her of all she'd lost?

"What's wrong?" Jeb asked, a frown on
his face, questions in his eyes.

"I was engaged once," she admitted,
the streaming water blurring as her eyes
misted over. "But that was a long time
ago."

Chapter Six

Jeb wanted to tell her he knew all about that engagement. But he couldn't find the words. He'd bring hurt to her either way. If he brought up John, and told her he was his kin, it would hurt. If he sat here and stayed silent and she found out later, it would still hurt.

"Do you want to talk about it?" he asked, deciding that staying neutral might be the best plan for now. He might not be here long anyway, and once he was gone, she'd never need to know.

Rebecca gave him a quick glance, then looked at the gurgling water that flowed through this small community. "What is there to say? We were engaged and about to be married. He was riding a horse, one his *daed* had just purchased and brought home. The horse was fidgety and skittish and a vehicle on the road backfired near where they were riding."

"It scared the animal," Jeb said, closing his eyes to the worst, and quickly opening them to see the horror in her expression She'd gone pale, her lips trembling.

She nodded, her hands held tightly together in her lap, her knuckles white against her blue dress. "I was there. I'd been watching him, my arms dangling over the fence rail." She shook her head, as if to get the memories out of her mind. "The horse lifted up and took off so fast, John lost the reins and… He was thrown. He landed too hard and hit his head against a fallen limb." She stood and stared at the water. "He…didn't wake up. I ran to him, and he wouldn't wake up. He was already gone."

Jeb tried to find air. He knew his cousin had died young, but he'd never heard the details. Her description was so close to what had happened to Pauly. "I'm so sorry you had to witness that, Rebecca. This is why you're afraid of horses?"

She bobbed her head. He stood up and moved close. "And this is why you never married?"

She whirled then. "*Ja*, how could I ever marry anyone when the man I loved so much died before we ever had a chance to be happy together?"

Jeb realized two things standing there, the scent of her milk-and-honey soap wafting out around him. She would never get over losing John, and Jeb could never reveal that he was John's cousin. He couldn't bring her any more pain when he wasn't even sure if he belonged here.

Father, what should I do? How do I pray for this woman? Help me see the way.

It had been a while since Jeb had turned to God. He'd cried out to God a lot, blaming the world for his problems, and railing at God for creating them. But he'd learned his problems were because of his own doings and the consequences of his choices.

But Rebecca, what had she done to deserve such a cruel turn of events? She'd say this had been God's will.

Why would God do that to her?

You're here now.

Jeb took in a breath. He *was* here now. When he'd seen the sign on the road and walked up that lane, weary and drained, he'd immediately felt a sense of home.

I am here now.

"Rebecca," he said, wanting to say so many things, "I'm sorry for that horrible loss. Sorry that you had to witness the death of the man you loved. You've done something remarkable, though. You've created a thriving business and made a life for yourself. A good life. You managed, even with tremendous grief, and you should be proud of that."

She wiped at her eyes. "*Ja,* I am content

most days. But… Remembering is never easy. Remembering what might have been, that gnaws at me and stays with me every day of my life. I know John is with *Gott* now, and that there has to be a reason why this happened. I will find out that reason one day."

Jeb almost reached for her but drew his hand back. He had no right to let her think they could be anything but friends. He was drifter, a wanderer, a lonesome soul. Lost.

And she was a beautiful soul. Lost.

Would it be so wrong to think they could be together?

Maybe not wrong, but first he'd have to find a way to help her forget the man she truly wanted to be with. John, the man who'd left her all alone.

And Jeb would have to make some life-changing decisions. Did he want to stay here? In his heart, he did. But his head didn't think he could ever be worthy of a woman like Rebecca. He should pour out his heart to her, tell her everything. But then she'd never trust him again. It might be too late for the truth between them.

Jeb decided he'd leave all of it in the Lord's hands.

He'd do the work, be a friend to Rebecca and try to show the world he could be more if she ever hinted as such.

But would she ever see beyond her grief? And could he be more to her, as damaged and doubtful as he was?

He glanced back at her. "Do you want me to catch that big bass?"

She laughed at that. "*Neh,* let him be. He's been around a long time." Then she looked into Jeb's eyes, her heart showing in that beautiful gaze. "But I will be happy to fry the fish you did catch."

"You mean, for supper?"

She nodded. "With me. I'm inviting you to supper with me. Would that be okay?"

Jeb thought that would be wonderful. "Yes, that would be great. I hate eating alone."

"So do I," she said. "Fish a bit more and

we'll go get things started. We'll have a feast out on the old picnic table under the oak."

"I'll try to catch another big one, but not Old Man Bass."

Smiling, she said, "I'm hungry. You might need to catch two." Then she headed back toward the house. "We can talk about our lilies. Next week, we start transferring them to pots."

Jeb could think of nothing better than a good meal with a pretty woman who loved to talk about lilies.

"This is so good," Jeb said after he'd eaten his fish. "Crispy and perfect."

"I'm glad you caught several," Rebecca replied. She poured more tea into his ice-filled glass. They'd fried potatoes with sweet onions and sliced the tomatoes. She had apple pie that Hannah had brought.

"It's a nice night," Jeb said when she passed him his slice of pie. "You have good spot to watch the sunset."

"I do." She told him the story of the two windows in the kitchen. "My *daed* was always so proud he could do that for my *mamm*. She was able to see most of the sunrises and sunsets, depending on the season."

"That was thoughtful," Jeb said. "So your parents were happy here."

"They were. We all were. They loved each other so much, and they loved us." Curiosity made her bold. "How about your family?"

Jeb put down his fork and looked out at the glow of pink and purple over the water. "My folks pretended to be happy, but they had a hard time of it."

Rebecca could see the deep pain and regret in his eyes. "I'm sorry, Jeb. Is that why you left?"

"I left for all the wrong reasons," he said. "I felt guilty after my brother died."

"Why?" she asked, figuring it had been hard for him to admit that.

He had to trust her. He knew he could,

but he wasn't ready to let go of his shame. "It was my fault."

"How can that be?"

He sighed and gave her a look of resolve, as if he knew she'd keep asking. "He looked up to me. Paul—we called him Pauly—had issues. I didn't understand at the time, and neither did my parents. But now, having been out in the world, I found some answers. He had a birth defect that left him with the mind of a four-year-old. He was sweet one moment and angry the next."

He stopped, his eyes on the flowing water off in the distant. "My *daed* would beat him."

Rebecca put her hand over her mouth. *"Neh."*

Jeb shook his head. "It's hard to understand. Mamm loved Pauly so much. She always said he was a special gift. He'd be young forever. Only after she died, he changed even more. We all did. Daed got worse. He stopped with the verbal abuse, but he shunned Pauly. It was up to me to take care of him."

"And you tried?"

"I did, but I was a teen. I had a job—we needed the money. Daed wasn't the best farmer." He took a sip of tea. "I worked at a buggy-repair shop not far from our house. I usually walked to work. Pauly didn't like being with Daed, so he'd sneak out and run away. Usually, he'd come straight to the buggy shop."

Rebecca put a hand on his arm. "You don't need to tell me the rest." She could imagine what had happened and she didn't want the details. Not yet. Not until he was ready to tell her everything.

Jeb let out a sigh. "Good, because I usually don't go further, even when I relive that horrible day in my nightmares."

She glanced at the creek and then back to him. "We share similar grief, ain't so?"

He nodded. "Becca, as Amish we learn that everything is *Gott*'s will, right?"

She nodded. "Correct."

"Do you ever question that?"

"I have, especially after I lost John."

"I did the same after Pauly's death. My *daed* and I never got along and being just the two of us—well—he used that to pick on me and blame me and tell me how worthless I was. So, I left. I've been running ever since."

Rebecca's heart caved in. What this man had suffered—no surprise why he had been roaming the earth in search of peace. "You find it hard to believe that could possibly be *Gott*'s will?"

He nodded, his eyes full of torment. "I've been wandering for twenty years. My entire family is gone now. Did God put me through all of that, knowing I'd wind up here one day?"

Rebecca wasn't sure how to answer that. Had the Lord let John die, so she'd be sitting here with this man one day?

Anger pieced through her heart. She wanted to get up and go into her house and shut all the curtains. Why did Jeb bring this out in her, this need to let go of her bitterness and sorrow and find joy again? She wasn't ready for joy again. Not the kind between a man and a woman.

She'd had enough joy living here alone. Hadn't she?

"Why do you think he brought you here, Jeb?" she asked on a sharp shrill.

"I've upset you," he said, standing. "And it's getting late. I should go."

"Neh," she said, her hand in the air. "Sit back down. You can't ask me something like that and then just get up and leave."

Jeb put his hands on his hips. "I shouldn't have shared all that and I know I asked a stupid question. I wound up here out of desperation."

"Maybe," she said, calming a little. "Why did you come here?"

He stared out toward the waning sun. "I've been to so many different places, some Amish and some *Englisch*. I guess because I'm getting older and I no longer have a home in Ohio, I thought I'd cross to the other side of Lake Erie and see what Lancaster County had to offer."

"It is one of the biggest Amish settlements," she said. "At least that's what the tourists like to repeat."

"Yes, and Campton Creek sounded perfect. Not too big and not too small. Beautiful."

"You did your homework on that, too."

He hesitated, then looked down at the ground. "I asked around, yes."

"So why would you ask me if *Gott* brought you here?"

"Look, it was a dumb question," he said as he started gathering dishes. "I got too deep. Never mind."

Rebecca stood back. She shouldn't push him when he'd been asking an honest question. "Jeb, we can't outguess the Lord. If He brought you here, He had a *gut* reason. But we'll have to see if that reason is ever revealed. Maybe He just wanted you to come home to your faith."

"Maybe," Jeb said. He went quiet as they gathered dishes and walked toward the house. "I enjoyed supper. I'll find my answer one day. I have to believe that."

After they'd placed their dishes on the old farm sink counter, Rebecca turned to him. "If you mean to stay in Campton Creek, I think it's time you go and talk to the bishop. He's a kind man who offers advice and wisdom. Were you baptized?"

"No. I left before I took that step."

"Then you'll need some preparation so you can go before the church and ask forgiveness."

"And then it will be over. I'll be a true Amish again."

"Ja," she said. "If that's what you really want."

"It is," he said. His eyes stayed on her for too long. "That and so much more."

Before she could ask any more questions, Jeb turned and headed out the front door. Rebecca walked around the kitchen, the last glow of the sunset glistening through the trees and beaming a good-night to the creek stream.

"Why did You send this man to me, Lord?" she asked before she turned out the lamps and went up to bed. That was the burning question now. A question she might not ever understand. Jeb had shown up out of the blue, but he'd also picked this spot, out of all the Amish communities in this area.

Did he know more about Campton Creek than he'd told her? Would he stay and become strong in his faith again? He sure was the best worker she'd had, but then she'd only had an older man before. He had not been inclined to talk, and he'd stayed out of her way most days.

Jeb had stepped into her heart from the moment she'd seen him strolling up the lane. She told herself she was only caught up in offering a stranger help and getting help in return, and she had to admit, because he reminded her of John, she'd been intrigued by him.

She needed answers in the same way she tried to figure out growing lilies. She had to have proof of what worked.

"I will keep praying for those answers," she told the Lord before she drifted off to sleep. Just like her beautiful lilies, Jeb needed to be cultivated and pruned a bit so he could shine brightly and find his faith, and so he could put down roots.

Chapter Seven

Jeb woke up the next morning still wondering why he'd blurted out his past to Rebecca. She was just so easy to talk to. He'd never felt comfortable around women, maybe because his father had not been a good example of how to treat women. His mother had tried to teach him to be kind and respectful of women.

"You are not your *daed*," she'd whispered one late night after his father had been on a rant. "You are a kind boy and I know you'll grow up to be a *gut* man. Kindness and respect will take you a long way in this world."

Jeb wished that to be true, but it wasn't in all circumstances. He'd tried so hard to forgive his father and turn the other cheek, but after Pauly died that had been almost impossible. If only he'd done the right thing that day.

After they buried his little brother, Jeb gave up on forgiving his *daed.*

He'd left his home believing that kindness and respect didn't always win out. He'd met some wonderful people out there in the big world, but he'd also met some cruel ones who would do anything to make others suffer. He didn't want to be that kind of person. When he gave someone his word, he kept it.

At least now he was home, and he had a job he really enjoyed, even with the hard work it required.

Even with the woman he couldn't help but be attracted to—his boss. Rebecca was kindness personified. An amazing woman. And so pretty at that.

Stop it, he told himself. He hadn't finished his story and he never would. Rebecca wouldn't want him here if she knew the whole story. The saddest part of that day Pauly had died.

Besides, Jeb was John's cousin, and he couldn't even bring himself to tell her that. Maybe that made him selfish, because he wanted her to like him on his own merit, not because he was related to the man she'd loved and lost.

I loved him, too. I just don't know how he'd feel about this. And Jeb sure didn't know how Rebecca would feel about him withholding something so important.

Jeb finished dressing and went to make breakfast. A knock on the door of the *grossdaddi haus* brought him out of his thoughts. He went to see who had come to visit this early in the day.

Noah stood there, dressed for church. "Are you ready?"

"Ready for what?" Noah asked, squinting into the morning sun.

"Church," Noah said, bringing himself on into the room. "I'll wait while you change."

"I hadn't planned on going," Jeb admitted. Amish church started early, around eight thirty in the morning, and lasted till noon. Jeb didn't mind that, but he wasn't sure if he was ready for being exposed to the whole community. Most Amish didn't judge and forgave easily, but just like the world out there and his *daed*, some did not.

"Oh, you're going, and you'll meet the bishop," Noah replied. "I mean—if you're serious about returning to your faith, of course."

Jeb wanted to be angry, but he was so confused he decided talking to the bishop might be for the best. "Is everyone in your family this bossy?"

Noah laughed. "*Ja*, better get used to it." Then he tugged at his Sunday hat. "I'll be waiting by the family buggy."

"The whole family?" Jeb asked, wondering if that included Rebecca.

"Sure," Noah said with a glint in his

dark eyes. "My wife and I and Katie. And Becca always rides with us to church. The boys follow on their bikes or horses. Don't worry, we've got room for you."

Jeb stood there after Noah shut the door. What was up? Noah forcing him to go to church and yet, knowing he'd have to sit in the buggy near Rebecca. Noah sure was in a hurry for Jeb to meet the bishop. Rebecca had mentioned that last night, too. While Jeb knew it had to be done, he'd rather meet and talk with Bishop King in private.

But Noah had not asked, he'd told. Jeb didn't want to start off on the wrong foot on a Sunday morning, so he changed into the black pants and white shirt Franny had given him, telling him he might want to go to church now and then.

"I guess it's now," he mumbled as he grabbed a dark hat, hoping it was the proper one for church.

He had not been to any church in a long time. He'd entered a few when they were empty, just to hear the silence. He loved the way a still, silent church felt, so safe and protective. He loved the scent of sweet flowers and burned candles, the perfume of a hundred blossoms left over by women who wore hats and used fans and walked around in their dresses and suits. Then he'd found other churches where everyone wore flip-flops and T-shirts and smelled like coconuts and pineapples. Where the women wore shorts and not much more than bathing suit tops. Some of the worst bars in Florida held church on Sunday morning. What was that all about? Maybe a bit of forgiveness for Saturday night transgressions?

The Amish didn't consider church as a building but rather a state of mind. That was why they held the service from place to place, home to home, moving around the community in a time-honored rotation. Jeb had missed that steady routine, too. It would be good to sit and listen to the old hymns and get acclimated to the old language, too.

He finished dressing and walked out into the warm morning, the buzz of bees humming in his ears.

He didn't have to look up to know what Rebecca would be wearing to church. But he couldn't keep his head down, so he took time to smile at her when she approached the buggy. Her green dress smelled fresh like her fields, the scents of sun and wind mingling with a slightly fragrant something. Peach, maybe?

"Jeb?" she asked, her eyes bright as he walked toward her. "Are you going with us?"

"Yep," he replied. *"Ja."*

She gave him a once-over. "Did Noah make you *kumm*?"

Jeb grinned. "Kind of, but he also told me I had to sit by you in the buggy, so I agreed on that stipulation."

She hid a giggle with her hand. "My *bruder* is so…difficult."

"He wants me to talk to the bishop, same as you suggested last night."

He saw fear in her eyes and a hesitancy. "What's wrong?"

"My *bruder*, going all around *me* to find someone for *me*."

Jeb shook his head. "I don't understand."

Her smile turned into a feminine pout. "Noah has decided to make a match for me—with you."

Jeb couldn't believe what he was hearing. Jolted down to his feet, he shook his head. "But Noah doesn't like me."

"I know," she said, whispering as the family came out to the waiting horse and the big buggy. "But when you told him you used to be Amish and you wanted to return, he got it in his head you'd make a fine match for me—his poor unmarried sister. Now he's determined to make that happen."

She must have seen his shock on his face. "Jeb, think nothing of it. I…we…can't listen to my misguided *bruder*." Shrugging, she said, "I won't let him force us into something we'd regret, and you shouldn't either."

Noah and Franny came out the door with Katie on their heels. Rebecca shot Jeb a warning glance. "Don't mention this."

"Are you two through passing secrets?" Noah asked, grinning. "It's time to go."

Jeb took the covered basket Rebecca held and placed it in the storage area of the open buggy. Then he helped her up onto the wide back seat. Katie jumped in between them. "Daed said I could sit with you, Aenti. He said between. Between."

Rebecca shot Jeb a wry smile. "Your *daed* always thinks of me, ain't so?"

Jeb wasn't sure if he should get in the buggy.

Katie nodded and grinned at Jeb. "I always get to sit with Aenti Becca, but never between before."

The three boys came charging out. "Getting our bikes," Michael called.

Noah nodded. "Do not be late. Stay right behind us."

His sons elbowed each other, scrambling for their bicycles, and took off ahead of the buggy. "We'll get a head start," Elijah shouted.

Katie giggled. "Can Jeb sit with us? Does he get on the side of me?"

"I can," Jeb said, thinking he still had a brain in his head after all.

Rebecca shrugged and mouthed, "Sorry."

He gave her a returning, "It's okay."

At least he was sitting close to her, even if Noah had forced his young daughter to be a temporary chaperone by stuffing the sweet child between them.

Katie, blissful and full of life, pointed out flowers and trees as they went along. Her chatter kept him from being able to talk to Rebecca.

But he was confused. Did Noah want him to marry Rebecca, since he was available and about to return to the fold? Or did Noah want him to bolt and run like the coward he was, knowing he couldn't marry her. That would break her heart, even if she didn't want to marry Jeb. She'd think she wasn't worthy of any man. Jeb told himself he couldn't fall in love with Rebecca. That would never work. He'd brought too much of his past with him, and he was withholding an important part of that past—the letters from John and his relationship to John.

Noah had backed him into a tight corner. Either get on with being Amish or get going.

And now, Jeb wasn't exactly sure which of those two choices he should pick.

Rebecca placed the container of roast beef sandwiches she'd made for the church meal on one of the broad tables the men had set up under the old oaks of the Weaver place. Jeremiah and Ava Jane made such a sweet couple. They now had four children, Ava Jane's older boy and girl, and now a younger boy and a baby girl. Their house was a four-square nestled on the property by the creek that Jeremiah's family had owned for generations. Jeremiah kept the place spic-and-span, and Ava Jane had made a lovely home inside the house and out. They often bought lilies to plant along the well-tended beds Ava Jane worked on all year long.

While Rebecca held joy in her heart for her friend, her own heart ached like a festering wound. Her brother schemed to pass her off on her employee. Jeb had looked so shocked earlier, she wanted to go home and curl up in bed. But Rebecca had learned a lot, being on her own. She had to be tough and gentle, determined and flexible, and she had to take care of the things no one else could tackle. She'd explain to Noah that he needed to stay out of her love life, or lack thereof. Neither she nor Jeb would be pushed into something so ridiculous. She'd make that clear to Jeb, too, so he need not feel obligated.

"Hi, Rebecca," Ava Jane said in passing. As the hostess, she had to be frazzled but Ava Jane handled it easily. "How are you these days?"

"I'm…all right," Rebecca replied. "My busy season is about to start, so I'm a bit preoccupied."

"I heard you found a helper," Ava Jane said, her blue eyes matching the perfect, cloudless sky. "And just in time, at that."

"I think everyone has heard about Jeb, both *gut* and bad." Rebecca placed napkins and utensils on the table. The men would eat first.

Ava Jane stopped bustling about and touched Rebecca's arm. "Jeb seems like a nice person. Jeremiah can sniff out anyone who's faking in the same way he can sniff out fresh cookies. He likes Jeb. And if you hired him, you must trust him, right?"

Rebecca nodded, thinking of how kind Ava Jane was. "You've heard the rumors?"

Ava Jane nodded, her golden hair peeking out from her *kapp*. Placing a plate full

of peanut-butter-and-marshmallow sandwiches closer to the other trays, she said,
"About him being Amish, even though he
came here as *Englisch, ja*." She scanned
the table, then, satisfied everything was
in place, turned back to Rebecca. "There
were many rumors when Jeremiah returned after being away for twelve years.
You can imagine how he was scorned and
judged. I was the one who judged him the
worst."

"And now you are happily married."

"*Ja*, over five years and still going." Ava
Jane ran her hand over the tablecloth. "Just
remember, *Gott* knows how things begin
and he knows how they will end. I've always admired your courage and your wisdom, Becca. Stay the course and forget
the *blabberwauls*." Then she leaned close,
"And don't let those who think you should
be married worry you. *Gott* has that figured out, too. Trust me on this—Jeremiah
and I are living proof."

"Denke," Rebecca said, touched that Ava Jane had been so honest with her.

Ava Jane nodded and whirled when one of her youngies screamed too loud.

Rebecca finished helping get the food out, her thoughts streaming along like the gurgling creek. She'd felt Jeb's eyes on her during the short buggy ride to church and then later, across the aisle through the hymn singings and the ministers preaching. She'd tried to focus on the sermon, but it had been extremely hard, knowing her brother wanted her to make a match with the first man who'd shown up to work for her. She was surprised he hadn't tried to finagle old Mr. Yoder.

She wished she hadn't blurted out Noah's grand plan for them, but she had to be honest. Now she'd probably frightened Jeb right out of being her friend.

Because she couldn't imagine him wanting to be anything more.

Chapter Eight

Jeb walked up to Bishop King and nodded. "I'm guessing you'd like to talk to me, sir."

The bishop smiled and shook his hand. "I'm guessing you are the one who needs to talk. And don't call me sir."

Jeb nodded. "When could we speak? In private?"

Bishop King chuckled. "Anxious?"

"I guess I am at that," Jeb admitted. "I had not planned to get going on this right away."

He didn't know how much the bishop knew about Noah's interference in this decision, but he did know that if he didn't do something to prove he was an honorable man, he'd have to quit his job and leave Campton Creek behind.

Leave Rebecca behind. Which he should probably do on his own. Just go back to wandering around like a nomad. Only he wasn't ready to go back out into the world, so he had to do this.

Bishop King motioned for him to move over to where a giant oak shaded them and gave them some space as people began to leave for home. The familiar sounds of horses being hitched up and buggy wheels squeaking mingled with children laughing and mamas calling. The spring air held a hint of warmth, a promise of summer, hope for a new beginning.

Jeb wondered if Becca was looking for him so they could leave. He wondered when he'd become so indecisive.

The bishop waited until Jeb gave him his full attention. "Why are you holding back on returning to your faith, Jeb?"

Jeb hadn't realized he'd been holding back, even though he obviously had taken a long time to reach this decision. "I'm afraid," he admitted, glancing around to see if anyone was listening. He figured everyone still here after church knew to steer clear when a newcomer and the bishop were standing alone and in conversation.

He was right on that account.

The bishop's shrewd dark eyes pinned him to the spot. "What are you afraid of?"

Jeb tried not to squirm under that solemn stare. "I've been away for twenty years." He explained the situation. "I don't have anyone left. I knew this place from a relative who is no longer with us, so I came here."

"And you like our community?"

"I do. I found work that I enjoy, and so far, everyone has been kind to me."

"That is our way," the bishop replied. "Are you willing to work on returning to *Gott*?"

"I never left God," Jeb said. "I thought

at times He'd left me, but I can see now He was there, but He was waiting for me to do what I needed to do." He shrugged. "He led me here, I think."

Bishop King's dark eyebrows lifted like curling fence wire. "You need to be sure."

Jeb took in a breath. It was now or never. "What is required of me? I was never baptized."

The bishop's smile held wisdom and kindness. "You'll have to do a refresher course on our ways—read the *Ordnung,* study your Bible and mind your manners. Once you've completed your learning, you'll go before the church and confess and ask for forgiveness and a return to the way of life you left. Your past will not be mentioned again."

Jeb didn't want to ask how long all of that would take. What if he decided to leave at the end of summer?

The bishop sensed his trepidation. "This is a firm commitment, Jeb. If you can't follow our ways, you won't be able to return. You will have to live in the *Englisch* world."

Jeb nodded. "I'm going to ponder what you told me. I knew as much but hearing it from you makes it real."

"Take time to think on this," Bishop King suggested. "*Kumm* and see me next week." He gave Jeb his address. "I have faith in you, Jeb Martin. I've already heard *gut* things about you."

"But if I go through with this, you might hear bad things."

The bishop touched a hand on his arm. "All the more reason to be reborn in your faith, ain't so?"

"Yes," Jeb said. "The very reason I've been roaming around. I didn't feel worthy of ever returning."

"*Gott* will be the decider of how worthy you are," the bishop replied. "I feel confident that he has deemed you so."

"I want that," Jeb said. He did want that. He turned and looked up for the first time. And saw Rebecca across the way.

She waved and he waved back.

Bishop King chuckled again. "I think you want a lot of things, young Jeb. God did bring you here. Now I have no doubt of that."

Rebecca didn't ask any questions on the way home, since Katie was back between them and chattering like a little magpie.

"Aenti, did you like the sandwiches? Peanut butter and marshmallow is my favorite. I could eat them all day long."

"I had a bite or two," Rebecca replied, giving Jeb a smile. "I enjoyed all of the food."

"I had peach cobbler," Jeb said to Katie. "It was sweet."

"My *daed* says I'm sweet," Katie replied.

"You are at that." Jeb looked over at Rebecca, making her wish she had children of her own.

Noah glanced back. "Katie, aren't you tired yet?"

"Neh," his daughter said. Then she yawned.

They all laughed at that, but Rebecca could see the tension in Jeb's face, even when he smiled. She'd have to talk to him about his meeting later.

Once they were home, Jeb and Noah went to take care of the buggy and horses, leaving her with Franny and Katie. "I'm going on home," she said, watching as the boys biked up to the house. After they hurried to do chores, she turned back to Franny. "I'm tired."

"I'm sure you're more than tired," Franny replied, glancing toward the barn. "Noah should mind his own business."

"He told you of his wild scheme, then?"

"He told me of his *wunderbar gut* idea," Franny said on a snort. "In his mind, anyway."

Rebecca shook her head. "He's forcing Jeb into something he might not be ready for. Being Amish again is a big step and he's been away a long time. That's enough in itself, but now my bossy *bruder* throws me into the bargain, too."

"I tried to reason with him, but you know how he can be," Franny said. She stooped to deadhead a geranium. "I'll try again. Don't let him force you or Jeb into something you don't want, Becca."

"I don't plan on that." Becca thanked her for the ride and then started toward home. She'd have to talk to Jeb some more tomorrow. Today, she was too weary to think about her interfering brother. She'd make sure she talked to Noah, too, but in private. She needed him to understand she was happy with things the way they were.

She went inside the coolness of her empty house, then cleaned and put away the casserole dish, made herself a cup of mint tea and decided to walk out to check the fields. It was her daily habit, to go back out and just…be still.

Gott would want her to be still and think things through. Then she'd have to trust Him. Not anyone else.

Just as the gloaming came in a wave of burnished sunset, the air became cooler, and the wind died down to a sweet melody that played through the trees. She stood by the lily field, thanking the Lord for His provisions, for her love of flowers and for sending her a helper who could keep up with her.

Rebecca breathed deep and accepted that she had no control over any of this. She'd have to wait on the Lord to show her the way from here on out. Jeb had come into her life when she needed someone to help her with her work.

But she had to wonder if he was meant to be here. When she looked back on the last few months, and the day she'd heard that her longtime employee would have to move on, she'd felt a sense of panic. But she also trusted that she'd know when the right person came along to replace him.

She'd known that day she'd seen Jeb walking up the road. She couldn't send him away when he desperately needed to be needed.

And she had so desperately needed someone.

Not just for these beautiful budding lilies, but for her own peace of mind, too.

She sighed, turned around to go into the house and saw Jeb standing there in her yard.

She'd take that as a *gut* sign she'd made the right decision.

Jeb had waited until near dark to go for a walk. That walk had brought him to Rebecca's backyard. Afraid Noah would see him if he came up the front lane, he'd snuck out through the woods like a thief running from the law.

But this place calmed him and gave him time to stop and think of everything that had brought him here. He wished John could be here, married to Rebecca, with children running around. Then Jeb could feel right, more at home again.

But John wasn't here. He was with God now. Guilt filled Jeb's soul. He shouldn't have erratic feelings for his cousin's girl. But he also knew marrying again after becoming a widow was not frowned on in an Amish community. More like, it was expected so no woman had to go it alone. Would John approve of him now, however? Technically, John and Becca had never married. And yet, it felt as if they had. It felt wrong, even when it felt right.

He saw Rebecca on the edge of the lily field. She looked as if she belonged there, like one of the slender, elegant lily buds that would soon be bursting with color. She was a burst of color, a taste of spring, a ray of hope.

Stop that mushy-head talk, he told himself. He cleared out his brain and walked toward her.

"What are you doing?" she asked, her voice breathless.

"I don't know," he admitted. "I needed

some air, and this is the best place to find that and some space."

"So, you decided to claim my favorite spots as your own. First the bench by the creek, and now my lily field?"

"I can leave." When she didn't speak, he turned, feeling at a loss.

"Jeb."

Her voice carried over the wind like a prayer.

He whirled back around. "I can leave. I mean really leave. Pack up and move on. That might be for the best."

"Is that what you want?" she asked, her tone low and full of that small question.

"I don't know," he said again. "I've never been this confused in my life."

"Are you warring with *Gott*, then?"

"I could be. I want so much to just be at home again, but is this where I stop? Is this where I need to stay?"

She moved closer, the last of the sun's glow set behind her like a painting. "I think home isn't a physical place. It's where you feel the most *at* home. It's a place inside your head, and your heart. But to be here, to be Amish, you will be making the most important decision of your life. I don't believe you left the Amish, Jeb. I believe you left a life that was not best for you. You couldn't save your *mamm* or your brother, Pauly, but you could save yourself in the only way you knew."

"To run."

"*Neh*, to walk away from everything and try to find some peace. And that action spanned twenty years and brought you here. This community could be your home, your place to live, your place that comes to mind when you think of home."

She was close now, so close he could reach out and touch her. He didn't. He stood a foot or so away, enjoying the lilt of her words, accepting the truth in those words, and accepting that he did feel at home standing here with her.

"I'm going to stay," he said, meaning it

now, knowing it now. "I'm Amish. I've been an Amish man lost in the world."

"You're not lost anymore," she replied, her eyes telling him the secrets she couldn't voice. He believed she wanted him to stay, but maybe she also wanted to deny that.

"No, I'm not alone but I still have many roads to walk before I can be completely at peace."

"You did talk to the bishop. That is a start."

"It is. I have to let him know if I'm committed. Now, after your words to me, I am committed more than ever."

"I'm glad," she said, her hands clutched over her apron. "I like having you around."

He smiled. "I like being around you, but Becca, we have to accept that before I can be true, I need to find God again. Then I'll work my way toward the other part of why I'm staying."

"And what would that be?" she asked, her breath held on the air.

"You, Becca," he whispered. "You make me feel this peace inside my soul."

She gasped and put a hand to her mouth, tears forming in her eyes. "I have prayed for us, Jeb. Prayed for you to stay and find your faith again, prayed for myself to accept what comes, if it is *Gott*'s will. I don't want you to be forced into something you'd regret."

Jeb's heart opened at the agony in her words. She seemed sure about her feelings. They could only be friends. "And I don't want that for you either."

"We need to let things take a natural course. Nothing can be pushed or rushed."

"I have the rest of my life," he said with a smile, thinking being a friend of this woman would be an honor and a blessing.

"So do I."

He turned then and walked back toward his little house. But he pivoted at the corner of her porch. "I'll see you tomorrow."

"I'll be here," she replied with a wave.

The sun settled for the night and the sky

turned to a deep blue shot through with creamy oranges and vivid pinks that made the whole horizon sparkle like a bright quilt over the trees.

Jeb walked home, a peace coming over him. He smiled and took another look at the beauty around him. He could almost hear a sigh going out over the land.

Chapter Nine

❧

"**I**'m here, Aenti Becca."

Becca looked up from her *kaffe* and toast to find Adam standing at the screen door, grinning at her. "Daed told me I get to help you all summer."

Even though her brother wanted her to make a match with Jeb, provided Jeb followed through on becoming Amish, he'd still sent Adam as a chaperone of sorts to work with her and Jeb each day. Now that school was done for the year, Adam needed to stay busy. Amish children had plenty of free time during summer, but they were taught chores and work all year long.

"Kumm," she said, tugging at his hat. "Did you have breakfast?"

He nodded. "Jeb is on his way. I saw him before I ran over." Her nephew tucked his straw hat low. "I like Jeb and if I work with you in your big garden, I don't have to muck stalls."

"A *gut* trade-off, ain't so?" She ruffled his long bangs. "I'll feed you and Jeb lunch, too."

He bobbed his head, joy on his youthful face. "What are we doing today?"

"Ah, today we'll start moving the harvest into the pots and containers I ordered a month ago. They're in the barn. We'll set up a worktable and get going. I'll be selling them on the road and also here on-site." She pointed out the window. I usually set up the potted plants just on the outskirts of the field, so customers might ask me to dig up more."

"And you do *gut* at the mud sale," Adam reminded her. "Two weeks from now."

"Ja, and I need to prepare for that, too.

You are a *gut* helper already, reminding me of that important event."

A knock at the back door brought her head up. "Jeb, *kumm* in."

Jeb nodded to her. "We have acquired a hard worker," he said, poking at Adam's arm. "Let's see how much we get done."

The twelve-year-old beamed. "I can outdo you."

"You think so, huh?"

Rebecca shook her head. "Don't make me regret hiring you two."

Jeb gave her a quiet smile, his eyes telling her nothing. Maybe it was a *gut* idea to have Adam here to break the tension and force her to focus on work.

"First, I need the big long table in the barn to be brought close to the house. Then I need the wheelbarrow and a shovel. Adam, you can bring the compost to and from the compost bed behind the barn."

"That stuff smells," Adam said, twisting his nose.

"That's because it's a natural mixture of food scraps and—"

"—manure," Adam finished, giggling. "I'll have to wash *meine* boots for sure."

"And your clothes," she added. "This is what we do. I know you'll be fine."

Adam grabbed a biscuit and headed for the door. "I'm going to find the wheelbarrow."

Jeb smiled after him. "He's a good boy."

"The best of the three," she said. "He's kind and sweet, while his older *bruders* are at that age where they think they know better than anyone."

"I remember that age," Jeb said after taking the coffee she offered him. "I was trouble from the get-go."

She wanted to ask him more about those days, but decided he'd talk about it if he wanted to do so. "I think we all have times in our youth we'd rather forget. Being a teenager is hard—that transition from child to adult comes with a lot of drama and doubt."

"Were you trouble, Becca?"

She gazed at him, wishing she could tell him how she'd felt when she was young. "I had my moments."

They finished their coffee, neither ready to give up any past indiscretions.

"Are you ready?" she asked.

"I am." He smiled and put on his straw hat. "Lily field, here we come."

They worked together in the morning sun, transplanting lilies from the ground to the pots. Jeb learned the names and varieties of each one. Becca showed him how a bigger bulb could produce a stronger plant and bring more blooms. She smiled each time she held a hardy bulb in her hands.

He smiled because she smiled. Adam worked back and forth bringing what they needed to get several different varieties potted.

"I pot a lot of what is called Asiatic lilies—Stargazers are one of our most popular ones. People can use them for cuttings, or they can take them from the pot and plant them in a cutting garden. A lot of hostesses like to have that as a separate garden, so they can have fresh-cut lilies inside and not bother their blooming lilies, which can return next year."

"The best of both worlds," he replied. "How deep should I plant these, then?"

She held up a clay pot and gave him the measurements and depth that would be best for the bulbs. "This one will work well for the section we're potting today."

"And we leave them along the back of the house, in the pots, until we're ready to sell them?"

She nodded. "*Ja*, but we water them often and let them do what they do best. Grow and bloom." Then she grinned. "Sometimes, I talk to them."

Jeb shook his head. "You are a constant surprise."

"Then you don't find me *lecherich*?"

He had to stop and remember the translation of that word. "No, you are not ridiculous. You're smart and you're passionate about your work."

She blushed and went back to work. "That I am. Let's get back to it."

"They love the sunshine," she said later, right after they'd had lunch underneath the great oak by her back porch. She kept glancing at the three-row-deep cluster of potted lilies lining the area by the porch.

"I think you love sunshine, too," he told her while they watched Adam playing with a stray dog that came to visit daily, but never stayed. Adam named the dog Lily since the little thing seemed to like catching varmints around the fields and in the barn.

"I do love being out in nature," she said, laughing at the tan-colored dog and Adam tugging at a thick string of old rope. "I especially love midsummer when the different varieties begin to fully bloom. It's like...a rainbow sent by the Lord. Heaven surely smells like this field in summer."

Jeb couldn't take his eyes away from her.

She glowed with the kind of contentment and hope that he'd longed for all of his life. She glanced back at him, her eyes going wide, and then she started laughing.

"What's so funny?" he asked, the lump in his throat making his words husky.

"These days, Jeb. They are so beautiful and so rare. I haven't smiled so much in a long time. But watching Adam and that little dog and having a picnic under my favorite tree with you—it's a blessed day."

"The best day," he replied. "I will remember this for a while to come."

Lily ran right into their picnic, then skidded to a stop when she smelled ham. Then she became pristine and sat to stare at them with begging brown eyes.

Rebecca threw a small piece of the meat out from where they sat. Lily took off and gulped it down in one bite.

"That's all you get until supper," Rebecca said.

Jeb was almost glad the dog had interrupted them before he said something he'd regret. Becca was a lot like her lilies. She needed to be cared for and she needed air and sunshine to keep her happy. Strong but delicate, she might crumble if he told all he already knew about her. He had envied his cousin back in the day. John's letters had held happiness, while Jeb's life had only held hopelessness. Now, the guilt of his feelings for Becca made Jeb draw back. It would be best if he never shared that time with her. John's letters would only bring her pain.

And Jeb's confession to her would surely do the same.

Adam finished watering the potted lilies and turned to Becca. "I only gave 'em a little water, just like you said."

"You've done a fine job today, Adam. Think you'll like doing this all summer?"

Adam bobbed his head. "*Ja*, for certain sure. I don't have to put up with my *bruders* nagging me, and Katie wanting me to play dolls with her. I like being here on my own."

Rebecca laughed at that. "Sometimes, it's *gut* to have a little time to ourselves."

Adam grinned and ran a dirty hand over his face, leaving a black streak. "Jeb is smart. He's showing me how to care for the horses—I mean—Daed has taught me a lot, but Jeb lets me do things right off. And he doesn't stand there watching every move I make so he can correct me."

Becca hid her smile. Her brother had a way of micromanaging everyone. She only knew that word from hearing her *Englisch* customers complaining at each other. Husbands and wives didn't always agree on how many lilies they actually needed to plant, but one customer had told her his wife worked in finance, so she liked to micromanage both her employees and her family.

When Rebecca had obviously looked confused, he'd whispered, "She thinks she has to oversee the whole family, and check every little detail, or we'll mess things up. Her staff fears her, but they get frustrated with all her suggestions and abrupt decisions. Me, I just love her anyway. She means well, most of the time. You know anyone like that?"

Noah had come to mind that day, same as right now. She'd only nodded to her customer and now she only smiled at Adam. "Your *daed* has a big heart and he loves you. Jeb has a big heart, too, and he likes having you around."

"I guess I am nice," Adam said so seriously, she did laugh then. "Jeb told me I'm *gut* with the horses."

Jeb might be training his replacement. That made her both happy and curious. Would he leave once he had Adam trained in all his duties? Had that also been part of her brother's plan if they refused to go along with his arranged marriage for them?

Maybe they were all micromanaging things around here.

"You are indeed nice and also kind," she replied. "Now, go wash up and we'll have cookies before you go home."

Adam took off toward the pump, little Lily trotting after him before she pounced at his feet, wanting him to play. He'd worked without complaining, so her brother had taught him some things about hard labor at least. Noah had never sent any of the boys over unless she really needed them. He had to depend on them to help with the milking and care of the livestock. Noah raised dairy cows and sold their milk. Franny and the older boys took care of the goats. Franny made goat milk soaps to sell. Rebecca always received supplies of the good-smelling soaps and lotions on her birthday or Christmas.

Franny had a regular shelf in Raesha Fisher's Bawell Hat Shop. While a crew made hats in the small factory behind the storefront, Raesha's staff sold local products of all kinds—the kind of genuine Amish products tourists loved. The shop carried Franny's soaps and lotions and took a small commission right off the top, but Franny got most of the profits. Several of the retailers around the community took in Amish products on consignment. Hartford Hardware always carried local foods and produce and handmade items, and also provided a garden section where Rebecca's lilies took center stage.

When Jeb walked over to help her finish tidying up, she told him about Adam's compliments. "He really looks up to you."

"I think that's good," he replied, his eyes going dark. "My little brother looked up to me, but I let him down when he really needed me."

She saw pain in that darkness. Jeb's guilt weighed him down. "You couldn't help the accident, Jeb."

He heaved a breath and gave her a longing stare. "I wish I could go back and change that day."

"What really happened?" she asked, hoping he'd trust her enough to explain.

Jeb glanced at the lily field and then back to her, his expression full of regret and torment. "Rebecca—"

"Hey, me and Lily found a lizard." Adam came running up to show them the squirming prize before Jeb could speak, and the moment was lost.

What secrets did he hide behind those compelling eyes?

Chapter Ten

They soon had a routine going. Potting, pruning, weeding, fertilizing, watering. Jeb loved the ebb and flow of the days, even as spring turned to summer, and the days grew longer and hotter. Customers trickled in and out and some days got really busy, but Becca handled her clients like a pro, and let him stay in the background doing the physical work, while she chatted with her returning buyers.

He liked to eavesdrop on her conversations regarding the lilies. He learned a lot this way, and he got to hear her sweet voice lifting out over the countryside.

"*Ja*, that one's okay. That blue mold on the bulb won't hurt a thing. And this is a *gut*-size bulb to replant in your garden. It will produce a fine showoff as the years go by."

"If you want fragrance, try the Fragrant Returns. It lives up to that name. Lemony and it reblooms."

"Now, Miss Amelia is a more creamy-yellow but with a nice mild fragrance, but one of my favorites is Lullaby Baby. It's a white-pink blushing lily with a sweet fragrance. It really adds to your garden."

She knew all the names, the history, the scientific names, the award winners, and the everyday ditch lilies that had started her on becoming a prominent master gardener.

Jeb thought of the blushing lily with the sweet fragrance. Did she think of holding babies when she sold that particular flower? It sure made him think of that—a surprise since he'd resigned himself to the fact that he might not ever be a father.

Pushing such thoughts away, he took a glance at the dark sky. Today, rain had kept the buyers away and forced her two bored employees inside.

On rainy days, he stayed in the barn, and Adam took to hanging alongside him. He showed the boy everything he knew about livestock, because Jeb wanted to earn his pay even if he didn't work much on bad days. Adam had a general knowledge since Amish youngies were trained from birth on how to care for their livestock. While Becca only had the two horses, they still required daily attention.

"We have goats," Adam said this morning. "But we have to watch them. Aenti Becca does not like them in her lilies. Besides, if they eat too many, they can get real sick, real quick."

"Huh, I thought goats were notorious for eating everything and anything they wanted."

Adam did a little head shake. "Most people think goats will eat anything. They might try everything, but they get picky when they want a real meal. Mostly they forage until they find something tasty. But they can destroy whole gardens before they decide. The deer love lilies, too. But Aenti only shoos them away. She loves the fawns and does, so she makes sure she leaves them some feed to keep 'em out of her plants. But the goats—she's not too fond of them."

"So no lilies for goats, and be kind to the deer," Jeb said, thinking he learned something new every day. "My folks never raised goats. Just a couple of cows and some pigs."

"Pigs are messy, and they slide right through your hands," Adam said, his tone one that showed he'd had firsthand experience with fleeing pigs.

Jeb liked to quiz Adam. The boy was smart. Plus, that took Jeb's mind off Becca and helped Jeb get to know people around here without actually speaking to them. "So how do you protect your goats and keep them from straying toward those tempting lilies out there?"

"We have high wire fences—the kind they can't chew through—and we feed them hay and some feed first thing each morning, while they're still in the paddock. That way they're full enough to roam around the big pen. My *daed* had to cut down all kinds of trees and shrubs—pines, rhododendrons, rhubarb, sumac, honeysuckle, any blooming or ornamental plants—just so they'd have a clear paddock and pen. We let them out there and they can't reach anything beyond what's healthy for them."

"You sure know a lot about taking care of goats."

"We learned the hard way, as Daed says. Lost a few goats to ferns and such. That's why Aenti Becca doesn't want them in her garden. It's bad for her plants and bad for the goats." He shrugged. "She might not like the goats, but she'd cry if anything happened to them."

"I'll keep that in mind," Jeb replied. He never wanted to make Becca cry.

"Look, the rain's stopped," Adam replied, grabbing his hat. "I'm gonna see what else I need to get done today."

Adam nodded, smiling at Adam's work ethic. "*Denke* for helping me clean the buggies." Then he said, "Hey, Adam, I have a project, but I want it to be a surprise for Becca. I want to build her a potting shed close to the fields. If I let you help, can you keep it a secret?"

Adam's brown eyes lit up. "*Ja*, I can keep a secret, even when my *bruders* do something I don't like. Course, they kind of make me promise to keep their secrets— or else. Just let me know when you're ready to get going." Then the boy pivoted around like a top. "Uh, how do you plan to keep something so big a secret?"

Smart. Jeb grinned. "I'm going to cut the boards and make the frames, piece by piece, here in the barn and maybe at your *daed*'s place if he'll let me. Then I'll ask your *mamm* and Hannah to take her some-where—a frolic or a shopping trip to town for an afternoon."

Adam's eyes brightened. "And we'll haul it all to the spot, and have it together be-fore they get back? Like a barn building, but smaller!"

Jeb nodded and put a finger to his lips. "Not a word."

Adam did a silent zip with his fingers. "This'll be so *gut*."

Jeb hoped so. He was anxious to start his secret project.

After all the hauling they'd done to pot several varieties of lilies, he wanted to save Becca some steps by creating a work building closer to the field. He'd make it enclosed with a window on each side, and with lots of shelves for displays and stor-age. But he'd create two big doors that could be opened wide, so customers could walk right up to buy their lilies. Later, he hoped to build her a small shed out by the road where she could be available there to sell lilies, produce and other products. He'd already altered a hauling buggy to hold more plants. It'd be easy to load one up and hitch a horse to take everything to the road. Her old wheelbarrow was about out of steam.

Those projects should keep him busy all summer. The more he worked, the more tired he'd be each night. So instead of lying there thinking about Becca, hopefully, he could fall asleep.

Becca had mended everything she could find, but the rain kept up. Now she'd turned to baking. Four loaves of bread sat cooling on the table. Two schnitz pies rested on the old sideboard, the scent of orange juice, cinnamon and the dried apples she'd boiled earlier filling the damp air.

She took her tea and stood looking out toward the fields. This had been a gentle rain, the kind that begged for a book to read and a hot cup of tea to sip. The drip-drip of the rain falling off the old roof soothed her soul, while the homey smells in her kitchen made her wish for a family of her own, so she could share the food.

She'd send some home with Adam if she could catch him. The boy shadowed Jeb like a young buck following a stag. As much as she'd objected to Noah sending Adam over so she and Jeb wouldn't be alone, she did appreciate Adam's willingness to work hard. Jeb could be a *gut* influence on the boy, considering Adam learned way too much of what not to do from his older brothers.

Jeb had been a great influence on her, too. He'd reminded her of John when she'd first seen him, but now, he was just Jeb. He still had the same build and the thick, dark hair that stayed unruly, but his features were harder, more jagged and craggy. Still handsome, but he wasn't John. Jeb Martin filled his own skin and his own personality very well. She could appreciate him for who he was, not because of the man he reminded her of.

She'd heard from Franny he'd had several visits with the bishop, but Rebecca hadn't pressed him for details. That was between him and the bishop. That meant, however, that he was serious about joining this community. She hoped and prayed for that, not because of her confused feelings for Jeb, but because he needed a home, and this community could be the perfect place for him. This job could be his as long as he needed it, too.

She turned from the window, thinking she'd have a quiet supper and go to bed early. But a knock at the back door brought her around. Jeb and Adam stood there looking sheepish.

"Ask her," Adam said, poking Jeb's ribs.

"You ask her," Jeb replied, grinning. "She's your aunt."

"We smell pie," Adam blurted. "And we're hungry."

Becca couldn't hide her smile. She let

them stew there on the covered porch for a while. Then she lifted one of the pies from the sideboard and deliberately let them see it. "You mean this pie?"

Adam bobbed his head. "Told you, Jeb. Schnitz." He touched a finger to his nose. "I have the gift of scent and I smelled cinnamon and orange, and a whole stew pot of apples."

Jeb rolled his eyes and glanced at Becca. "Well, I have the gift of a grumpy stomach. That looks and smells delicious, whatever you put in it."

She laughed and motioned them in. "Wash your hands and make sure your boots are passable."

"We checked our boots," Adam replied as he almost knocked Jeb out of the way to get into the kitchen. "And Jeb makes me double-wash all over every day."

Becca sniffed. "You both smell clean enough. Have a seat and I'll pass the pie. Jeb, would you like *kaffe* or milk?"

Adam lifted a hand. "Milk is real *gut* with schnitz pie."

"Then milk it is," Jeb said, his gaze moving over Rebecca's face.

She blushed, thinking she'd missed him. This visit was a surprise and a joy. She didn't even mind that Adam was with him. She'd send pie home with her nephew. Really, she was almost glad Adam had come inside. She could be with Jeb, but not be alone with Jeb. Because her heart might do something stupid like make her flirt with the man if they were alone.

His eyes told her he might be thinking along the same lines. That, or he really just wanted some pie.

Jeb enjoyed every bite of the pie. He enjoyed watching Rebecca even more. She moved around her kitchen like a dancer doing a choreographed waltz. When she turned and saw him staring, he lowered his head. "This is really good. I haven't had schnitz pie in many years." He glanced out the window. "I think this crust is even better than my mother's."

Adam's head shot up. "Jeb, why did you jump the fence?"

The question, asked with such earnest curiosity, threw Jeb, and surprised Rebecca.

"Adam, do not be so nosy."

"It's okay," Jeb said. He'd give the boy the honest truth. "I was mad at the world, and I think I was mad at God, too. I had a bad home life. Then I lost two people that I loved."

Rebecca shot her nephew a warning glance. Adam looked from her to Jeb. "I'm sorry, Jeb. I reckon that could make anybody mad."

Jeb fought against the lump in his throat and the hot mist forming in his eyes. "I shouldn't have blamed anyone," he said. "And I shouldn't have stayed gone for so long."

He pushed the pie plate away, leaving a big chunk of crust.

He didn't tell the boy that he blamed himself more than anyone for not taking care of the two most fragile people in his family—his mother and Pauly. He failed them...and his father, too, in every way.

"I'd better get home," Adam said, giving Rebecca a worried glance. "Did I ask too many questions? Mamm says I'm too chatty for my own good."

Jeb stopped the boy with a hand on his arm. "You did nothing wrong, Adam. I enjoy our conversations. It's just difficult to talk about those who've gone on before us. But take this as a lesson from me. Never abandon the people you love. Family is more important than anything. Remember that."

"I will." Adam swallowed, his eyes going wide. "I hope you can stay here and be part of our family, Jeb. I sure do like you. And... You make Aenti Becca smile."

Then he grabbed the extra pie Rebecca had cut and wrapped and turned to head out the door, leaving Jeb to stare over at

Rebecca. "Is that true? Do I make you smile?"

She wiped at her eyes and sank down across from him. "Most of the time, *ja*, but right now I just want to cry. You've been carrying a heavy burden, Jeb. Don't you think it's time to let it go?"

Jeb stared over at her. He wanted to let it go, so much. He wanted to let it all go, tell her the truth, and then take her in his arms and hold her tight. He wanted to feel the goodness and pureness that flowed through her, needed it to cleanse his sins and his soul.

Instead, he stood. He had to get out of here before he made a big mistake. He couldn't blurt out the truth. Not yet. "Thank you for the pie. I'll see you tomorrow."

Then he went out the door and walked home in the gentle rain, his sins still burning at his soul.

Chapter Eleven

Noah was home when Jeb got there. Normally, he'd dread seeing Rebecca's overbearing brother, but today he needed to talk to him.

"Noah," he called, thinking if he started his secret project as soon as possible, he'd feel better about everything. "I need to ask a favor."

Noah waved him into the barn since it was still sprinkling rain. Once Jeb was inside, Noah stood staring. "What do you need?"

Jeb explained what he wanted to do for Rebecca. "I thought I'd work on it here, mostly so Rebecca won't see it. Then we'll ask Hannah and Franny to get her out of the house for a few hours, so we can bring in people to help put it together while she's away."

Noah gave him a confused stare. "That's a mighty ambitious project, but she does have a birthday coming up. Do you have enough lumber for such a project?"

"I found some in the barn and it's in good shape. I might have to add a few pieces, but it's not going to be a big shed. Just a place where she can work—like a greenhouse."

Noah's fierce stare didn't evaporate. "Why are you doing this?"

Jeb felt the fire of that stare. "Because she needs a shed close to the field. She wasted a lot of steps yesterday and today, going back and forth with plants and pots. I tried to fix the old wheelbarrow and it's not going to do. She shouldn't have to stoop and bend all day long when she can have a nice place with shelves and stools and a whole wall full of any kind of tools she might need."

Noah burst out laughing.

"Is this funny to you?" Jeb asked, anger and frustration mounting. Was he wrong to want to make Rebecca's whole operation more efficient?

Noah put a hand on his shoulder. "You really do care about her, ain't so?"

Jeb shifted on his work boots. He might have known Noah would get the wrong impression. He'd never understand the man. "Of course. She's my boss and she works hard. Adam has been a big help, but honestly I don't know how she did this with the old man she told me about being her only helper most of the time."

"I've encouraged her to hire more help, even offered to help her pay for it, but my sister likes her solitude and the quiet," Noah replied, serious now. "I'm glad you want to do something nice for her. How are the lessons with the bishop going?"

And there it was—the reason Noah was so pleased with this idea.

"We aren't talking about me," Jeb replied, wishing everyone would stop trying to pair him with Rebecca. "I need your permission to use the barn and I'd like to borrow some of your tools to plan out the shed pieces and have them tagged and ready so we can get this built. Adam wants to help, and he's promised to keep it a secret."

Noah laughed again. "Did he, now?"

"He promised."

"I'll speak to him." Noah glanced around, then turned back to Jeb. "My sister lost the man she loved before they were married. Right before they were to be married. She's never quite recovered. I don't want her to get hurt again. Understand?"

"I do understand," Jeb replied. "More than you'll ever know." Then he got bold. "But explain to me, if you're so worried about her getting hurt why are you insisting that I consider marrying her?"

Noah looked surprised and then he looked sheepish. "Well, she has a lot of love to give, and she needs someone who can match her, step by step. I keep my eye on her, as you well know, and it irritates her to no end, as you've probably noticed. I'd rest better knowing she has a *gut* man in her life. You fit the bill, except for you needing to reaffirm your faith, of course." Noah paused and let out a sigh. "I know I've been hard on you, but this is what I mean—if you and Becca become close and then you just up and leave, she'll be devastated all over again."

Jeb could see the love and concern in Noah's eyes.

He looked over at Rebecca's house. "I like the work, Noah. It's helping me in more than just financial ways. A good day's work makes a man feel worthy and hopeful. I won't mess that up by hurting the woman who was willing to give me a chance. The only person in the world, really, who was willing to give me a chance."

Noah stayed silent, his hands holding to his suspenders, his dark eyes solemn. "I will help you build the potting shed, as a gift to my sister. We will make sure it's a surprise." He shrugged. "And I have some lumber here in the barn that needs to be put to *gut* use. If you need more, let me know. I'll buy some at the lumberyard in town."

Jeb breathed a sigh of relief. "I'll pay."

Noah gave him an appreciative stare. "No, you're doing enough. Sometimes, Jeb, the thought is worth much more than the cost."

This would cost Jeb a little bit more of his heart, which he was willing to give. But Noah's warnings still rang loudly inside his head. Could he follow through and stay the course?

He prayed he could, and he would talk to the bishop about his fears and concerns.

"*Denke.*" Jeb nodded and shook Noah's hand. "I'm glad we've come to an understanding. I want this to be a work shed

Rebecca can use every day. I believe she will find the shed efficient and accommodating."

Noah chuckled and hurried toward his house. Then he called back, "I have no doubt she will appreciate it."

The next week was a busy one as the whole community prepared for the upcoming mud sale. Jeb helped neighbors put finishing touches on the things they wanted to sell at auction and also helped set up the grid for the sale to run smoothly.

On Saturday, Jeb and Adam loaded up the hauling buggy with potted lilies and a few other perennials and took off to the third sale of the season. Rebecca, Hannah and Franny had all kinds of foods and crafts to showcase, and Noah had some farm tools to be auctioned, so Noah packed the family buggy with their wares, including two quilts to be auctioned off, too.

Noah had told Jeb this particular sale went toward the volunteer fire department, and since several Amish men volunteered, the whole countryside came to show their appreciation. "It's like a big festival, with food and celebrations."

"I heard Becca and her sister talking about the quilts they'd made."

"Some of the quilts go for hundreds of dollars," he'd said. "The *Englisch* get intense about handmade Amish quilts."

Jeb had liked Campton Creek from the moment he set foot in the quaint little township. Everyone here from the *Englisch* to the Amish had been kind to him. He didn't mind helping to pay it back somehow. He might even volunteer himself.

Soon, the two buggies were heading into town, where the sale would be held in the big park by the creek, Jeb and Rebecca in front with Noah's family following.

While the horse trotted leisurely, Rebecca explained how the town came to be and pointed out the Campton Center, which used to be a private home. Majestic and big, the brick house with the grand white columns took center stage on the main thoroughfare. The *Englisch* Camptons were the original founders of the town and still had relatives here. Judy Campton, the matriarch who had lived in the house, was now in an assisted living facility that she'd funded to be built not far from here. It served both *Englisch* and Amish. But her friend and assistant Bettye still lived in the carriage house apartment and often helped out in the offices.

The house and grounds were pretty, but he rather enjoyed looking at Rebecca. She wore a light green dress that matched her eyes, and her hair was perfectly parted down the middle, not a strand out of place underneath her shining white *kapp*.

"A lot of people have been helped there— with legal issues, heath issues and financial issues. They serve the Amish mostly, but anyone in need is welcome. You might see Jewel running around. She's the manager and... Well, she's a bit eccentric but she has a heart of gold."

"I take it this Jewel person is not Amish."

"Neh." Rebecca giggled. "She used to be a bouncer at a bar, and she went through a lot—drugs, assaults, depression. But she got herself well of all that and now she likes to say she's high on Jesus." When he frowned, Rebecca added, "Jewel is one of those rare people who loves everyone, no matter their flaws. So, we in turn love her back."

Jeb listened in awe, wishing he had someone in his life to love him unconditionally. He had the Lord. He knew that and Bishop King had encouraged him to remember his faith, to breathe it and accept it, rather than trying to force himself onto it. "Let the faith grow from your heart, Jeb. Don't pretend. That won't work. You have the foundation, but you lost your way. You'll know it's in your heart the minute you accept *Gott*'s love fully back into your life. Your heart will burn with such joy." Then the bishop had smiled. "And you will be worthy of that joy."

Jeb could feel a burn right now. It happened each time he glanced at Rebecca. The day was beautiful and bright, with low humidity and the kind of spring breeze that made a man feel alive. And hopeful. A new life, a new beginning.

He felt it, all right. And he thanked the Lord for providing such moments. But how could he ever be worthy of such hopes, of a new beginning? He wanted so much, but he couldn't risk hurting Rebecca. She loved John, still loved John, or she would have married by now.

He'd not told her the truth—about John—and about what had truly happened the day Pauly died. Jeb's hope sank. If he were to be honest with her, Rebecca would send him packing.

He'd have no new beginning. Just another tragic ending.

Rebecca wondered about Jeb. They'd been laughing and talking, then he'd gone quiet on her. She'd noticed that about him.

Sometimes, he'd go to a place in his mind, a faraway place. The place where he kept his secrets and his pain.

She wished she could help him, but she had her own dark times, her lonely times full of regret.

She wished they could help each other.

Lord, I pray You will show us the way.

Her silent petition on their part would stay between *Gott* and Rebecca. As they pulled up the wagon full of plants, she turned and checked to see if Noah and Franny were behind them. Katie waved to her and smiled. Rebecca waved back, then she looked over at Jeb. "Are you ready for this?"

"As ready as can be. I'll do whatever is needed."

"Is something wrong?"

"No." He gave her a crooked smile. "I guess I'm feeling homesick and missing those I love."

Ah, that would explain his sudden quietness. "They are safe with *Gott* now. And you are here on earth, on this fine day. I hope you have *gut* memories of today."

He gave her a soulful smile. "I think I will."

"Everyone is here and accounted for," she told Jeb. "The boys came early in the summer buggy to help set up. We hope. Those three manage to get right into trouble just standing still."

"Adam says his brothers keep him in trouble."

Rebecca couldn't argue with that. "I think that's part of why Noah sent him to help us. That and the poor youngie is a distraction for us."

"Oh," Jeb said, back to smiling. "Do I distract you from your work?"

She gave him a quick glance and caught the smile he tried to hide. "At times, yes."

After they found the big open booth where they'd set up their plant nursery, he laughed and hopped down to get the horse situated. Then he started helping her unload the plants. "So, I'm a distraction," he reminded her. "So are you at times."

Rebecca shook her head. "We are so concerned with distracting each other that it's becoming another distraction. Why don't we just accept that we are friends?"

Hiding his disappointment, he said, "I thought that was a given."

She pursed her lips in a teasing way. "I need something official."

He grinned. "I took this job because I needed money and a purpose. You've given me that and more. I'd like to be your friend."

"Then you are my new friend, Jeb."

"Ah, then call me Jeb, the way you've been doing."

"And you call me Becca, the way a friend should."

They stood with a white lily between them. An Easter lily.

"To new beginnings," Jeb said, watching how she held tight to the plant.

"To new sunrises and sunsets," she replied. Then she sniffed at the lily, her eyes closed in bliss, her smile shining a light on his heart.

Jeb had never wanted to kiss a woman so badly, but he stood and took in the lemony scent of the lily, along with the sweet perfume that seemed to surround Becca.

That joy burned another warm thread through his heart, a thread that warred with the secrets of his soul and bound him to this woman forever.

Chapter Twelve

Rebecca's nursery booth stayed busy all day long. She could hear the auctioneers calling out, their gavels hitting against the podium each time an item was sold. Hannah came to help and told her their quilts had sold quickly.

"Both went to sisters who live next to each other in Florida. They were so happy to get them and know that sisters had quilted them together. One loved the wedding ring quilt and the other had to have the tiger lily." She poked Rebecca's arm. "When I told her how you'd made it and also grow lilies, she said they'd come by here soon."

"The threads of life," Rebecca said with a smile. "They flow through all of us. It's nice to know what we created together might be shared with their daughters one day. Or that lilies I grew will grace their gardens."

Hannah glimpsed at her, then waved to an Amish couple as they strolled by. "You're sounding wise, sister, but I think I hear a bit of resolve in your observation."

"I'm not wise, just beginning to see more and more how we're all connected. But I am resolved. I have to remember I am content, and *Gott* knows my future."

Hannah moved some colorful pots of Gerber daisies closer to the front row so customers could see them better. "Does this resolve have to do with the man over there loading lilies into that tiny car?"

Rebecca glanced to where Jeb moved back and forth to help Jewel place several White Lemonades into the trunk of Jewel's vehicle. Jewel planted a new garden of lilies just about every year at the Campton Center. The ruffled, creamy lemonade flower would open early with lush, hardy blossoms, and it tolerated the winters.

"It might," she admitted, after considering her sister's question. Keeping her voice low, she watched Jewel and Jeb having a lively discussion. "Jeb and I had a *gut* talk on the way here. But I don't expect him to stick around, even if he does become Amish again."

"Where would he go?" Hannah asked. "He says he likes it here."

"Onward," Rebecca said while she fussed and plucked at her plants. "He's a wanderer."

"Might he settle one day, if he found the right place and the right person?"

"That's what I have to be practical about," Rebecca said. "I have to accept whatever *Gott* has planned for Jeb. But I'd like it if he stayed. He and I have reached an agreement. We will be friends."

Hannah almost snorted but held her hand over her mouth instead. "Friends? Well, that's so practical I can hardly stand it."

"Don't tease," Rebecca cautioned. "There can never be more between us, and I must accept that."

"Because you have feelings for him?" Hannah asked, surprised.

"Because he needs a community and *Gott* back in his life," Rebecca said. "That is his priority right now. But… I do like him. A lot."

"Does he know that you like him a lot?"

"Shh, he's coming back. Of course not. I can't tell him anything when I'm not even sure myself. Now, hush up and help me line up the Stargazers."

Hannah nodded. "*Ja*, while I try to ignore those stars in your eyes."

"Who has stars in their eyes?" Jeb asked from the corner.

Rebecca shot her sister a warning glance. "I do. We should make a fair amount of money and be able to contribute more this year to the Volunteer Firemen's Fund."

"A good cause," Jeb said. "I talked to Jeremiah Weaver about joining up."

Her sister smiled at Jeb. "You're settling in nicely, ain't so?" Hannah's voice held that mischievous tone Rebecca knew so well.

"For now, I'd say so," Jeb replied, his eyes on Rebecca. "I'll go find us a quick lunch. Anything in particular you'd like, ladies?"

"The roast beef hoagies are great," Hannah said. "I'll have one of those."

"I'll take a chicken salad sandwich," Rebecca told him.

"Okay, I'll be back soon with that and some drinks."

"I can give you some money," Rebecca offered, digging through her tote bag.

"No, my treat," Jeb replied. "My boss pays me well."

They all laughed at that, but after he

strolled away, Rebecca gave her sister a playful slap on the arm. "You are so bad."

"I can ask a person a simple question," Hannah replied with a smirk.

"It is interesting that he's thinking about becoming a volunteer fireman," Rebecca said, her gaze following Jeb as he greeted people.

"So interesting," her sister teased. "I think Jeb's wandering days will soon come to end. Think about how many people come here, some to come home, some to hide away from the world, but most always stay."

Rebecca shook her head. "I have given this over to the Lord, sister. If Jeb stays here, it will be *Gott*'s will, and it will have to be Jeb's decision. We are friends, and that will have to suffice."

She wouldn't hold him back from moving on, because she wasn't sure she could give her heart to anyone again. No matter how much Jeb made her feel as if she'd already lost part of that heart.

* * *

"Aenti Becca, I bought a doll," Katie said as she rushed up to Becca's booth.

The little faceless doll wore a light blue dress and tiny apron. It had no face because the Amish believed everyone was alike in the eyes of God. They didn't believe in graven images of any kind.

"That is a pretty little doll, for certain sure."

Katie swayed and hummed. "I named her Becky after you. Mamm said that name is a lot like Becca."

"Well, that's mighty sweet of you," Becca said, giving Katie a hug. "Where have you been all day?"

The crowd had dwindled to just a few strollers, and she only had a few potted lilies and plants left. It had been a nice day.

"I had to stay with Mamm," Katie said, shrugging. "She fretted about me getting lost. My *bruders* don't like me tagging along."

Her cute pout only reminded Rebecca

of the days to come. Katie would be a heartbreaker one day. Rebecca wished she could prepare her sweet niece for the hard parts of growing up.

"Does your *mamm* know you're with me now?" she asked Katie.

Katie danced back and forth with her faceless doll. "Uh-huh. She watched me and said to *kumm* straight here and stay put, while she cleans up and gets ready to go home."

Becca glanced down the way and waved to Franny. Her sister-in-law nodded and waved back. Franny's thoughtfulness in allowing her children to spend time with Rebecca made her thankful, but also hit her with a bittersweet pain.

Thinking about John, she remembered how kind and sweet he'd been, always with a smile or a joke. He made her laugh. He made her want to be a better person. She'd dreamed of the day they'd have a child together. When she lost him, her world had gone dark and even now, she preferred being in the shadows. She craved a quiet life. But lately, she'd become restless, her heart yearning for something she might not ever have.

Jeb had changed her way of thinking and lightened her loneliness. He'd brought their lunch and sat to eat with them, in between customers. Hannah helped there while they finished their meal. The food fulfilled Rebecca's hunger, but each time she glanced at Jeb, she thought again of how much she'd lost. She could never forget John. But Jeb was different—world weary and aged, but still handsome. He'd brightened in both spirit and looks since the day he'd come walking up to her house.

Thank You, Father.

Now, she began to pack up her plants, handing them off to him one by one, so he could carry them to the waiting buggy. When he returned for another round, Katie showed him her doll.

"That's nice," he said, glancing from the *kinder* to Rebecca. "My *mamm* used to make those dolls. She only had boys, so she'd give them to her friends for their daughters."

"You didn't have a sister?" Katie asked, surprise shining in her eyes.

"No, just a brother."

"Where is your *bruder*?"

Jeb looked at Rebecca, helpless on how to answer.

"Katie, do not pester Jeb. He has to finish his work."

"Can I help?" Katie asked, on to another scattered thought.

"Why don't you put Becky here by my tote," Rebecca said, giving Jeb a quick glance. "Then you can carry the small herb pots back to the wagon."

"Okay." Katie carefully lifted one clay pot of mint. "I'll be so careful." Then she tiptoed her way to the buggy.

Jeb smiled, then let out a breath. *"Denke."*

Rebecca nodded. "She is inquisitive."

"As she should be at that age."

He grabbed more pots and hurried to the

buggy. Soon, he and Katie were in a deep conversation about butterflies.

But Rebecca could see the darkness falling back over his features. He somehow blamed himself for his brother's death. She prayed he'd be able to talk to the bishop about that and hand it over to the Lord. Sometimes, forgiveness didn't *kumm* easy, especially if a person couldn't forgive himself.

She had a feeling Jeb would not quit wandering until he could do that very thing.

Katie managed to get permission to ride home with Rebecca and Jeb, but she didn't squeeze between them. She sat in the back with what was left of their supply of plants.

"I like lilies," she said in a singsong voice. "Consider the lilies of the field..." Katie went on humming and talking to her doll. "My *aenti* grows pretty flowers. She has a gift."

Rebecca shot a quick glimpse toward Jeb and smiled. "Her *mamm* teaches her Bible verses in both Deutsch and *Englisch*," Rebecca whispered. "She is a good learner."

"She is wise," Jeb replied, his gaze on Rebecca for a moment. "God takes care of the lilies of the field and all creatures."

"He does, indeed." She settled back, tired but content, the lingering scent of Easter lilies—*Lilium Longiflorum*—wafting out around them. "He gave us such a beautiful earth. I'm honored to be able to work with His world."

"We had a profitable day, didn't we?"

She nodded. "*Ja*, better than I'd expected." Then she added, "*Denke* for your help today."

"Just doing the work you pay me to do."

"You will receive extra for the overtime."

He took a glimpse at her as they turned the big buggy onto her lane. "Then I can buy you a meal again."

"Or I could cook us a meal, to celebrate."

"That would work."

They dropped Katie off and watched for traffic as she crossed the road and ran home, Noah waiting for her with a smile.

"Your brother didn't even fuss at me today," Jeb said after they'd unloaded the few remaining plants from the buggy. "He kept me busy, though, probably so I wouldn't spend too much time with you."

Rebecca had seen Jeb helping out wherever he was needed. Noah would call him to do a favor in his stall, then send him to take over for someone else so they could go on a break. Noah's way of getting Jeb involved in the community, and it seemed to have worked. People had commented to Jeb each time he helped load pots and flowers onto their cars or vehicles.

As they pulled the buggy up to the stables, Rebecca turned to face Jeb. "Well, my *bruder* isn't here now, is he?"

Jeb gave her a look that told her about many things without him saying a word. Then he leaned toward her. "Are you saying you want me to stay and visit for a while?"

She glanced at the dusk. "The sun is about to set. It would be a shame to watch it all by myself."

Jeb looked from her to the creek. "I wouldn't mind seeing the sunset. Let me get the animals settled and I'll meet you back there."

Rebecca watched as he hurried to the barn.

Now, why did I do that?

She should have said good-night and sent Jeb on his way.

But as much as she loved watching the sunsets to the west, she hated sitting on that bench alone.

Would it hurt to enjoy just a few more minutes with a man who had become her friend?

Chapter Thirteen

Jeb hurried with taking care of the horses and made sure the chickens were fed. Since Rebecca had no other animals, he made quick work of his chores, then washed up at the pump near the barn. He was tired, but in a good way. He'd met a lot of nice people today. Some frowned at him, but the bishop had made a special visit to their booth to talk to Rebecca and him, probably to see how they acted around each other.

"You are a great help to our Rebecca, Jeb," Bishop King had told him after buying two bright yellow lilies.

Jeb thought about how this place settled him and kept him calm. It would be hard to leave if he did decide to do that. Rebecca made each day so easy, and he had meant what he told her. He wanted to stay in Campton Creek. But wanting and doing were two different things. And even the best plans could change in a heartbeat.

When he came out of the barn, he saw her sitting on the bench, the old oak nearby shading her from the last of the sun's rays. She held a small tray with lemonade and two small plates of what looked like cake.

"What do you have there?" he asked as he approached. She smiled and scooted over.

"I had one loaf of apple bread left. Thought we could have a bite."

"That's nice. I like apple bread. But then, I've never turned down any food you've offered, in case you haven't noticed."

"I have noticed. *Gut* thing I like to bake."

He took the glass of lemonade and a

chunk of the moist cake. "You are a kind person, Becca."

"*Denke.* I could say the same about you."

He chewed another chunk of cake, wondering what she'd think if he blurted out all his secrets and fears. "I have not always been kind. Bishop King has helped me to find a way to let go of all of the things holding me from my faith."

"Such as?"

"Anger, bitterness, regret and my need to fight starting over in a new place."

"That's a lot to let go of and straighten out." Rebecca gave him an earnest appraisal. "Would you like to tell me why you're so angry?"

Here was his opportunity to come clean, but Jeb held back. They'd had such a nice day and he didn't want to ruin it now. "I guess I'm angry about my home life not being so good, and that I tried my best and still failed. I seem stuck in the past, but I can't go back to fix it."

"You can't blame yourself for everything, Jeb." She sat silent, her hands in her lap. "When you're ready, will you tell me more about Pauly and what happened to him?"

She wanted the truth. He needed to give her the truth. "I want to tell you everything, but could we just be friends while we sit here? Could we enjoy each other's company and this evening?"

"I did say whenever you are ready," she replied on a soft whisper. "I want you to know you can tell me anything and I won't judge you."

He nodded, his appetite gone, his fears like talons clawing at his skin. "I'll remember that."

They finished their apple bread, and she set the tray down on the grass. Then Rebecca did something that made him wish he could be honest with her.

She took his hand and held it in hers while the bright yellow orb of sunlight slipped over the trees and the whole sky glistened and shimmered in a cascade of pink and purple.

As the last of the sun's rays descended, Jeb knew one thing for sure. They had gone past the friendship mark.

Something more was going on with them now.

The next week, Jeb started on cutting the boards to build the potting shed he'd planned out for Rebecca. She rarely came into the barn, so he managed to saw several boards and number them before he stacked them in a corner.

Adam ran back and forth to alert Jeb if Rebecca was nearby.

"She's hanging wash."

"She's hoeing the vegetable garden. I'll go help and distract her."

"She's playing with Lily. That dog likes the treats she bought for her at the general store."

"Aenti Becca walked over to see Mamm. We're in the clear."

Today Jeb stepped out of the barn with Adam, since he'd just reported Rebecca had gone with his *mamm* to see a sick neighbor.

"Okay, so we'll measure the square footage underneath that old live oak that borders the corner of the field closest to the house. I've already cleared the ground since she doesn't want weeds growing on the edge of her garden."

"She's mighty thankful for that," Adam told him.

"But you didn't let anything slip, right?"

"*Neh*, I'm not going to spill the beans. Mamm and Daed know, 'cause I heard them talking about it the other night. Daed told me if I ruin the surprise, I'll have to clean the chicken coop for a month."

Having cleaned a few chicken coops, Jeb could commiserate with the boy. "Try not to mention it when she's around," he said. "You've been a great help. On Saturday, after half day, we'll work in your *daed*'s barn to build the frame for the roof."

Adam bobbed his head. "Then we just tote it over here and frame it up. Only after Mamm and Hannah take her to town."

"That's the plan," Jeb said. "Now let's measure this ground to be precise."

They hurried and figured out the dimensions and Jeb wrote them on an old slab of wood he kept out of sight.

They finished and went to prune the herb box so Rebecca would have fresh herbs to dry and some to use in her cooking.

By the time she came home, they were done with work and fishing at the creek.

She marched out and did a quick inspection, glancing over the growing lilies, then back to the vegetable garden, then the herb box.

"We did it all," Adam called. "Everything on your list is finished, Aenti."

"That's *wunderbar gut*, Adam. You can go home early."

Adam shook his head. "I wanna catch some fish first."

Jeb sent Rebecca a big smile. "He's already caught two nice breams."

"Okay, then," Rebecca said. "I have things to do in the kitchen. I will talk to you later."

Jeb waved and watched her walking toward the house, Lily Dog at her feet. It was a beautiful picture to see her there beside the blooming lilies, a dog dancing at her feet. A homey, welcoming picture.

One he thought of every day.

Since she'd held his hand the other night, something had changed between them. They were shy at times and laughing at other times. He had to wonder if this was what it felt like to fall in love. He smiled more, had more patience, tried hard to please Rebecca, enjoyed his talks with the bishop and slept better every night.

It could be the work and the sunshine. Or it could be the food and fellowship. But Jeb knew in his heart, he was changing because of Rebecca's sweet disposition and her tolerance of a stranger showing up on her doorstep. Rebecca showed people grace and kindness, things he'd not always had at home or out in the world.

But this week, he'd felt a shift in her that concerned him. Did she feel the tug and pull of feelings, just as he did? Was she fighting those feelings, too?

After Adam went home, Jeb lingered to water some plants and hopefully see Rebecca again.

She finally came out on the porch. "All done for the day?"

"I think so," he said, noting she looked tired. "How about you?"

"I'm done here. We had a good crowd this morning. Thank you for taking the buggy of plants up to the road. I sold all of them." She studied her blue sneakers. "I like the bench you fixed and placed up there. I can sit and read while I wait for any customers."

"Well, you are welcome, but you don't have to sit there in the sun all day."

"*Neh.* I only sell there during heavy traffic times—morning rush is a *gut* time to catch people."

"Is there such a thing as morning rush in Campton Creek?" he teased.

"*Ja,* it gets a little busy now and then," she retorted with a smile. "A lot of buggies heading out for the day."

They laughed together, then Jeb asked, "Rebecca, are we okay, you and me?"

"What do you mean?"

"Are we friends?"

"*Ja,* but why do you ask?"

He couldn't blurt out his feelings, so he said, "I would never do anything to upset you."

"You haven't."

He wasn't handling this right. He tried again. "You held my hand the other night. It was nice."

Realization colored her eyes. "Oh, I did, didn't I?"

Jeb waited.

"I enjoyed holding your hand, but Jeb,

you know how it is. We have to be careful. Noah is always watching."

"Noah had nearly given us his blessings."

"But he has to be sure... And I have to be sure."

"I see. You're all waiting for me to fail?"

He turned to leave, but she ran down the steps. "That is not what I said. Noah might be waiting for that, but I'm not."

"But you still aren't sure about me?"

"I'm sure of you, Jeb. I'm just not so sure of myself."

"Well, the same goes for me," he retorted, holding his disappointment tight. "I reckon we can keep working on it."

Rebecca gave him one of her soft smiles. "We are like those lilies out there. Growing, changing, blossoming. A work in progress."

Jeb wasn't sure he liked being compared to a flower, but he did see one correlation between himself and the lilies. "I aim to put down roots, Rebecca."

"*Ja*, and that's *wunderbar gut*," she replied. "But the question is—will you put down roots here or will you keep wandering and try again somewhere else?"

"I'm talking with the bishop weekly. Doesn't that prove something to you?"

She smiled again, which only made him more agitated. "It proves you are working hard to find your way home—to your faith. You can take that with you anywhere as long as you're truly back among us."

"Or I keep my faith right here in Campton Creek and be a content man."

Her next smile held a bit more mirth. "And that would make me a content woman, Jeb."

"Right now, you are a confusing woman," he retorted. But he said it with his own smile widening. "I'm going across the road now, Becca. See you tomorrow."

"Good night, Jeb."

He chuckled and waved as he walked away, the glow of their banter giving him new hope, even while the old fears pushed at his heart. He'd find a way, some way, to stay here and he'd also find a way to tell her what he'd held on his heart since the day she'd let him into her kitchen.

He wanted to spend the rest of his life as near to Rebecca as he could be. If that meant just being her employee, he'd have to accept that and consider it a gift from God.

Chapter Fourteen

As summer progressed, Rebecca's field of lilies grew and developed, the scent of the blooms filling the air from dawn to dusk. She opened her bedroom window as night settled over the yard and gently sloping hills. The scent of the lilies, along with the magnolias her *mamm* had planted years ago, and a few gardenias she'd managed to keep in pots and bring in during the winter, surrounded her. Inhaling, she thanked God for his beautiful world.

But summer also brought tourists, and today had been a busy day. Some just stopped to take pictures of the symmetric rows of lilies covering the countryside in shades ranging from white to lemon and orange, followed by reds and burgundies and deep purples. She tried to plant her lilies so the lighter shades would show off and lead to the deeper shade. It made for a beautiful field, almost like a colorful quilt.

She also mixed up a few in a special area, so they could hybridize and produce new variances. Most people came to buy but weren't sure where to begin or how. The mixed garden gave them an idea of which colors worked together. It had become a popular new addition to her garden.

Jeb had suggested she have pamphlets made up, explaining the basic steps of planting, growing and hybridizing the exquisite flowers. He'd helped her draft a sample, and he'd taken his design to the Campton Center where Jewel studied it and created a mockup on the fancy laptop that she used to keep the center running.

Jewel had delivered the big box of pamphlets this morning.

"See what you think, Rebecca," the sturdy woman with short, cropped hair and dangling red earrings had said, her smile shining bright with joy. "I had so much fun designing this for you. I found stock photos online and bought us a few. I even came to your field the other day when you'd gone visiting and snapped some photos. Jeb had a great idea with the handout information. That one, he's a keeper. Hardworking and easy on the eye."

Jewel had winked when she'd said that, causing Rebecca to blush. "He sure brags on you," the eccentric woman had whispered. "I think he's got a big old crush on you."

"We are friends," Rebecca tried to explain. "But I do appreciate his knowledge on such things. I never thought to create a pamphlet on growing lilies. I can hand them out, rather than repeating myself over and over. Progress."

Jewel, wearing a bright floral long tunic over blue jeans, had agreed. "Jeb is smart. You let me know when these run out. I'll order more."

"How much do I owe you?" Rebecca asked.

"It's paid," Jewel replied. "The man who has a crush on you covered the tab, but don't fret. I gave him a supergood deal." Another wink, which Rebecca interpreted to mean Jewel had saved Jeb from giving up too much of his pay.

Now as she stood looking out at the moonlit field, which showcased her moon garden lilies nicely, she felt a bittersweet ache in her soul. Her loving parents were gone to heaven, up there with her beloved John.

But she was still here on earth, and a new man had come into her life. A confusing, complex, tormented man who seemed to be running from himself more than from the world. Yet, he'd stopped here, had come to her door begging for work.

And he'd done a lot of things to improve her little farm. He worked with the horses and cleaned and polished everything from the bearing reins to the saddles and back straps and fixed up broken buggies and even the old wheelbarrow. He'd cleaned and organized the barn and he planned to repaint it when things settled down after the spring rush.

So many little tasks she'd neglected, Jeb had found and taken care of. He never complained and he loved having Adam around. Did Adam make him think of his own brother, Pauly?

Rebecca closed her eyes and prayed to the Lord to help her make her way through this maze of feelings that shifted and shined in the same way her lilies did. Why did she feel this pull toward Jeb? Her feelings had gone from a soft pastel to a deep burning fire red. What was she to do?

She had no answers. She'd have to wait on the Lord with this predicament. But it was hard to wait sometimes.

She was about to go to bed when she saw a white flash moving along the outer row of lilies.

A goat.

Rebecca grabbed a shawl and ran down the steps and out into the yard, her hands flapping, her shouts sounding over the night. The big billy goat ignored her as he sampled some of her prettiest Farmer's Daughter circular-shaped blooms. Rebecca screamed and stomped her foot, but the old goat ignored her.

She went closer, hoping to scare him. "Get away. You'll be sick."

Then she heard footsteps running behind her. "Rebecca!"

Jeb. She whirled and motioned to him. "Old Billy's out and he's messing with my Farmer's Daughters."

Jeb went to work. He ran to the barn and came back with a broom and hurried to hit at the goat. The animal lifted his head and hurled his body toward Jeb, but Jeb was ready. He sidestepped and slapped the

broom lightly on the goat's backside, causing the animal to careen away and back
toward the pen from where he'd obviously
escaped.

Jeb ran up to Rebecca. "Are you all al-
right?"

"*Ja,*" she said, out of breath, her braid
of hair slipping over her shoulder. "I don't
want him to be sick. He rules the roost
over there."

Jeb glanced at the road, and then turned
back to her, a smile cresting his face. "But
he ruined the Farmer's Daughters."

Rebecca realized the implications of
what she'd shouted out, then she smiled,
too. Soon, they were both laughing so
hard, he held her arms to steady her.

"I suppose that did sound strange," she
managed between giggles. "But he'll be
the one to pay. He's going to be sick."

"I'll find him, and I'll let Noah know
what happened," Jeb said, still snicker-
ing. "Do we need to check on the...uh...
Farmer's Daughters?"

They started laughing again. Rebecca shifted to turn and hit a stump. She went right into Jeb's arms.

Jeb stopped laughing, his eyes on her, his breath coming in huffs. "Rebecca..."

Rebecca's heart burned for something she couldn't describe. A need, a longing, a wish.

He leaned in and pulled her head to his, his hand on the thickness of her braid. Then he put his lips on hers and kissed her in a slow, sweet, lingering way that had her sighing into the moonlight.

She didn't want to let go, but logic took over. She pulled away. "I... I should get inside. It's late."

And her hair was down, her head bare of her *kapp*. She still had on her old work dress, but her apron was in her room.

Jeb nodded, his eyes dark in the grayish-white light. "I'll go find Old Billy."

They both stood still.

"Rebecca?"

"*Ja?*"

"Do you regret me kissing you?"

"*Neh*. Because I kissed you back."

"I noticed that," he said, his smile showing.

She tugged her shawl around her. "I might just thank Old Billy on that account, but I won't forgive him for ruining, I mean, tearing up my lilies."

Jeb grinned again. "And I will always remember the name of that particular lily."

He walked her back to the porch. "I might want to kiss you again, just so you know."

Her heartbeat raced, her pulse hummed, her hope soared. "And I might let you, just so you know."

She went back inside and checked her field again. No more goats. If Old Billy had broken out, more might come.

But Jeb and Noah would take care of that.

She wondered if Jeb would mention he'd helped her scare the ornery goat off her property.

He surely wouldn't mention what else had happened.

Jeb had kissed her in the moonlight mist. And she'd liked kissing him back.

The next morning Noah showed up on her doorstep.

"I'm sorry about Old Billy getting out. The fence near the edge of the goat pen has been damaged, probably from him trying to break out. It's fixed and he's gonna be okay, but he had a bad upset stomach. Doc King came to check on him this morning."

Samantha Leah King was the only female veterinarian in this part of the county, and she was also the only Amish vet available for miles around. She'd returned to the fold a year or so ago, after surviving a tornado and criminals trying to silence her, and married Micah King. They lived on the other side of Campton Creek on Micah's farm, where she had an office and kennels out back.

"I'm glad he's okay," Rebecca said as she

guided Noah inside and gave him a cup of coffee. "I hurried the moment I saw him out there."

"Jeb told me."

"*Ach*, is that why you're here?" she asked, giving her brother a questioning glance.

"He told me he heard you screaming— that he was sitting on the stoop at the *grossdaddi haus*."

"Do you believe him?"

"I do," Noah admitted. "I'd seen him there when I was making my final rounds, but I didn't bother him. A little while later, I heard shouts and then I saw him sprinting across the yard. Before I could get to him, I saw one of the nannies trying to break through. I had to go and fetch one back and get the others and the kids settled. I'm surprised they didn't all escape."

"Did he bring Billy back?"

"*Ja,*" Noah said. "And told me what had happened."

"You didn't come to fuss at me, or warn me against him?"

Noah let out a sigh. "*Neh*, and I was wrong on that account. I can see he's a good, trustworthy worker, but he is still an outsider, sister."

"He's trying, Noah. At your request. Don't pressure him."

"Are you afraid he'll leave?"

"I'm not afraid. I know he'll leave if you keep pushing him. Let it be. *Gott* will show him the way. You move between forcing us together or wanting him to just go. None of this can be your doing, or mine. It's Jeb's decision." Then she touched Noah's arm. "*Gott*'s will."

Noah's dark eyes softened. "I will stop, then. You need to understand, I only want the best for you."

Rebecca put her hand over his. "Then let me be, *bruder*. I'm content and I'm fine. Jeb is an honorable man who still knows our ways, even if he's been out there on his own for a long time."

"You'll wait to see if he follows through?"

"I know he's following through. He

meets with the bishop once or twice a week. He's learning and he's willing to return to us."

"To us?"

Leave it to her brother to misinterpret her words.

"To his Amish ways, and to *Gott*."

Noah finished his coffee. "He helped me last night and I will remember that. He's a big help to you—so I will consider that. I have no quarrel with Jeb if he does what he's saying he wants to do. Either staying or going, he'd best do right by you, too."

Rebecca stood and took their empty cups to the sink and pumped some water over them. "Then we both need to let him do his work and finish what he's started. I have faith that Jeb will make the right decision."

"We cannot make it for him, as you say," Noah replied, nodding, his hand tugging at his beard. "I'm sorry I've tried to arrange things to suit *mein* self. I had *gut* intentions."

"I know you had the best intentions," she told her brother as he stood and tugged at his straw hat. "Now let's find out Jeb's intentions and *Gott*'s intent."

After Noah left, Rebecca got ready for another busy day. When she heard Jeb and Adam laughing and talking, she watched them from the kitchen window. Jeb carried a huge blue umbrella and a white chair, heading for the lane.

She moved from the back window to the front and watched, amazed, as he dug a small hole at the end of the lane, near her sign, and placed the umbrella's pole into the earth and secured it with some boards and big stones. Adam, grinning, then opened the bright blue umbrella wide.

Jeb had made her a better place to sit when she sold lilies and herbs on the side of the road. Adam put a small ice chest down beside the umbrella. She guessed it held water and other drinks.

Rebecca sat down and accepted the tears

rolling down her face. A simple gesture, a thoughtful surprise, from a man who wanted so much to be seen, to be loved, to be a part of something.

"Please stay, Jeb," she whispered. "But not for me, *neh*. Stay for yourself, and for your faith."

She said a silent prayer to the Lord and asked Him to guide Jeb, and to help her. She wanted to be a friend to Jeb, but now she knew her feelings had changed to something more.

She wasn't ready to admit what that something was, but her heart burned like a field of dirt in the stark sunshine.

Rebecca remembered how she'd felt with John. This felt much the same, but different. Stronger, intense and overwhelming.

Did she ever really know this kind of love before, even with John? They'd been so young. Now, she was a mature woman who'd witnessed births, weddings, life and death.

Her feelings too overwhelming to think

about, she wiped her eyes and went out to thank Jeb and Adam for this thoughtful gift. She could never tell Jeb whom he reminded her of. That would put a wedge between them and make him think she was only being kind because he seemed so familiar.

"What have you two been up to so early in the morning?"

Adam beamed. "For you, Aenti. Jeb says you don't need to sit in the hot sun. I'll sit here and help you sell your lilies while he takes care of anyone wanting to see the field. It's our new Saturday morning tradition, ain't so, Jeb?"

"That's right," Jeb said, nudging Adam with his elbow. "We'd better get started, huh?"

"*Ja*, I can't have any slackers around here," she teased to hide the tremendous emotions rushing over her like the creek's gurgling waters.

But when her gaze met Jeb's and he smiled his soft smile, her thoughts settled into one realization. She was beginning to care about him as more than just a friend. It might even be love.

Chapter Fifteen

Jeb stood with the men at church the next Sunday, watching across the way for Rebecca to enter Noah's big barn. After the ministers had entered, the married men came next, then the married women. The single men filed in, so Jeb fell into place, being one of the older single men. He kept his eyes on the open doors. When Rebecca walked in with the other single women, she shot him a quick smile, then lowered her gaze. The younger girls and boys then entered. The men removed their hats and soon the service began.

As they sang the old hymns in High German and without music, Jeb thought about how he would eventually have to stand up in church and ask for forgiveness so he could return to the Amish way of life. Here in Campton Creek. He'd been happier here than he'd been in his whole life. Rebecca was a big part of that happiness, but there was more. He felt at home here. This place seemed to bring people home, to reunite families and sweethearts, no matter their flaws, or the past, or their secrets. Maybe some of that goodness would rub off on him if he stayed. Being around Rebecca made him want to be more faithful, more truthful, more focused on community and Christ.

But before he could do any of that, he would have to tell Rebecca the truth about his relationship to John. Her John. Would she understand why he hadn't told her from the beginning?

He couldn't even understand it himself, so how could he make her see his reasons for keeping that from her? It had come time to reveal his secret to the bishop. He couldn't honestly confess without telling the bishop and Rebecca about the letters John had sent him, especially about the last letter he'd received from John telling Jeb he was to be married. It would look like he came here purposely to find Rebecca, but he'd come here because his cousin loved this place.

Then God had dropped him right into Rebecca's world.

Coincidence or God's—*Gott*'s—will?

After the service, the men ate sitting on benches set up underneath the old oak trees by Noah's barn, not far from where Jeb stayed in the smaller house. Jeb went to sit with Jeremiah and Micah, two men he'd already become friends with because Rebecca knew their wives, Ava Jane, and Samantha the vet, who some called Leah, the name her grandmother called her.

A couple of other men showed up, their gaze hitting on Jeb with curiosity.

"Where'd you come from?" an older

man named Shem asked. "You remind me of someone."

Jeb lowered his head. He didn't want to lie. "I grew up in Ohio, but I moved around a lot, doing odds and ends."

"But you've been in the *Englisch* world, correct?" another man asked. "We don't get a lot of Martins around here."

"*Ja*, I've been moving around for a long time but I'm more Amish still than *Englisch*." Then he added, "My *daed* was a Mennonite. My *mamm* stayed Amish, and he… He tried to be Amish."

"There is no trying," Noah said as he settled next to Jeb. "Jeb here is going through the steps of returning to his faith—completely." He sent Jeb a determined smile.

Jeremiah laughed and looked at Noah. "I had to study with some youngies while working on the process of getting back to my faith. If I can sit and take the teasing I had to endure, I'm sure Jeb will make it all the way through."

Micah nodded. "Leah, as most of you

know, had to do the same. She had been out in the world for a long time. But she fell right back into her Amish ways, although she did have to get approval to continue her veterinarian practice."

"We are all thankful for that," Noah added with a chuckle. "She is really *gut* with the animals."

Jeb smiled as the stories were told. Then he leaned toward Jeremiah. "I'm thinking of volunteering as a firefighter."

"We can always use another hand," Jeremiah said. "Let me know and I'll give you a tour of the station *haus*."

The conversation moved on, but after they'd eaten and now stood mingling, the older man who'd questioned Jeb before came up beside him.

Shem Yoder grinned at him. "Minna Schlock married a Mennonite close to thirty-five years ago. I know 'cause I had a crush on her. That might be who you remind me of, except I can't remember the man's name."

Jeb's heartbeat danced out of control. This man remembered his mother. He was about to come up with an answer when Noah called him to help with packing up the buggies.

"I must go," he said, nodding to Shem.

Shem stared after him for a moment and then turned and walked away. But Jeb had a feeling this was not over yet. He'd need to tell Rebecca the truth, and soon.

Two days later, Noah found Jeb inside the barn back at Noah's house. "Can I speak to you about something?"

Jeb lifted a long board and turned to Noah. "*Ja,* what is it?"

Noah let out a sigh. "Have you been completely honest with us about your reason for coming here?"

Jeb's heart accelerated into a high beat. "I believe I've told you all the important stuff."

"Shem Yoder thinks he knows you."

Jeb looked down at the board he'd been

staining for Rebecca's potting shed. He worked here most afternoons when he got done with his paying work. Today, he'd loaded enough lily plants for the many buyers streaming in to make him never want to see a lily again.

But he did want to see those lilies, Rebecca's field of beautiful flowers, again. He wanted to finish this project and see how she'd react to it. He wanted so many things.

"He mentioned something about that to me Sunday," Jeb replied. "I'm not sure what's he's talking about. I could look like someone he knows."

Noah's shrewd gaze stayed on him. "Shem has a *gut* memory for his age. He says you remind him of a girl he walked out with, until a man named Calvin Martin, a Mennonite who was just passing through, took her away."

Apparently, Shem's memory had returned, or he'd done some asking around.

Jeb couldn't lie. Noah had begun to trust him. "Calvin Martin was my *daed*, Noah."

Noah looked surprised, then he became angry. "So, you did *kumm* here for a reason. But you couldn't have lived here before."

Jeb stopped his work and laid the staining rag down, then wiped his hands. Turning back to face Noah, he heaved a great sigh. "I never lived here. My *mamm* did, but she left when she was nineteen. She and my *daed* got married and moved to Ohio. Her family was not pleased that she'd married a Mennonite."

Noah let that soak in. "You grew up in Ohio, so that much is true, at least."

"I did, but I did not have the best childhood. I had a brother named Pauly. I've told Rebecca most of this."

"Except the part about your *mamm* being from here," Noah retorted.

Jeb decided to come clean. "There's more, Noah."

"I was afraid of that. You'd better get to the truth, Jeb."

They leaned back against the work counter, the soft hot wind of summer washing over them, the sounds of animals snorting and birds chirping making this seem like an ordinary day.

Jeb felt anything but ordinary.

"My *mamm* had a sister," he began. "Aenti Moselle was a bit younger than my mother, but they were so close. Aenti Moselle visited Mamm a lot, but she married a man who lived here in a nearby community. Emmett Kemp. They settled here in Campton Creek and had two children, a boy named John and a girl named Sadie."

Noah frowned. "The Kemps. Moselle was your *aenti*?" Gasping, he stepped back. "John Kemp was your cousin?"

Jeb nodded, his eyes burning with a hot moisture. *"Ja."*

Noah got in his face. "What are you doing here, trying to take his place? If Becca finds this out—"

Jeb held up a hand. "I didn't know, Noah. I did not know who she was until she'd already hired me. Then she told me her full name."

"But you did recognize the name? How?" Noah's face reddened with anger. "You didn't live here, and your grandparents have passed on. John's parents took Sadie and left. So how did you know to find her?"

"I didn't come here to find her," Jeb replied, trying to make sense of it. "I came here because John and I were close, and we visited each other when we were boys. Mostly he and his *mamm* would come to Ohio to visit. My *daed* didn't like to travel." He took off his hat and ran a hand through his hair. "John and I wrote to each other secretly for several years—because my *daed* didn't like my *mamm* getting letters from home. The last letter I got from him came just a few weeks before he died. He told me about being engaged to the most beautiful girl in the world."

Noah gasped again. "Rebecca. She was

so in love with him, and I don't think she's ever recovered from seeing him being thrown from that horse."

"She told me about it and her fear of horses," Jeb said. "She knows most of what I've told you. Seems we both are still grieving things."

"But you have not told her the truth of you being John's cousin. Now I know who you remind me of—John. Almost like twins. Your mothers weren't twins, but they resembled each other, ain't so?"

Jeb nodded. "They were like twins and *ja*, they looked almost the same, but after a few years, my *mamm*'s health went down. They looked nothing alike by the time she died."

"I'm sorry for that," Noah said. "What happened in your home, Jeb?"

Jeb let out another sigh. "Alcohol. My *daed* drank too much and took his sorriness out on my mother, Pauly and me."

He explained his life to Noah. But still,

he couldn't bring himself to talk much about the day Pauly died, or how he'd died.

When he finished, Noah stood staring at him, the sympathy in his eyes as clear as the anger he'd held earlier.

"And you say you've told Becca most of this?"

"I've told her everything but…me being John's cousin. I wanted to tell her a hundred different times, but Noah, I like my job and I mean Becca no harm. I was afraid I'd add to her pain and make things worse for her."

Noah studied him, shaking his head. "I don't see how she missed you looking so much like John. I'm surprised she's never mentioned that to you."

"It might be the same as me never bringing him up. Too painful."

"And she might have held back because she wouldn't want you to compare yourself to him," Noah replied.

"I'm nothing like him," Jeb admitted. "I left after Pauly died and I never looked back. I didn't make it home in time to make peace with my *daed*. I was too bitter and angry. I regret that, but I can't go back there. This was the place that stayed in my head. I still have some of John's letters. But I don't have much else."

Noah patted him on the shoulder. "First, you talk to the bishop, and then, Jeb, you talk to Rebecca. She believes in honesty above all else. You must tell her the rest of your story." Then he stood back. "Or I will."

Chapter Sixteen

Something was bothering Jeb.

Rebecca watched him now while he moved through the field alongside her, checking for spider mites and slugs. She had natural products to help combat pests, but it was a constant battle. Her lilies were hardy and resistant to most anything, but they had to be checked for every little thing. She liked pampering her crop. She'd explained this process to Jeb, and since he'd worked in fields before, he knew what needed to be done.

But he wasn't joking with her as he usually did or talking to Lily Dog in a low sweet voice, or mentioning Noah fussing at him about something, their usual work-day banter.

Did he regret kissing her?

That thought popped into her head, coming from a place where she'd buried her own feelings about their kiss. She'd loved kissing him, but she'd also accepted that it was wrong. He'd lived out in the world, and now he was forbidden until he'd finished his sessions with the bishop.

Jeb must have buried his own feelings deep, too.

He was pulling back, shutting down. The kiss had made him realize he couldn't stay here. He didn't want to give her the wrong impression. He didn't want to hurt her or bring shame on her. That was Jeb, always trying to do the right thing.

So noble. But neither of them could deny the intensity of being in each other's arms.

Those thoughts played through her head as swiftly as the wind played through the hundreds of blossoming lilies.

She was so lost in thought, her heart hurting while her head decided this was for the best, she didn't hear Jeb calling out to her.

"Becca?"

Rebecca stood and found him on the far side of the field by the woods. He motioned for her, so she started out at a trot to reach him.

He was in what she called the breeder plants section, seedlings that could be used to breed new plants even though the seedlings hadn't been given a name themselves. These were used to hybridize, and she usually suggested them to customers who wanted to experiment with cross-pollination.

When she ran down the slope of the hill, she saw why Jeb had called her. Half of that row of plants and some nearby had been destroyed.

Jeb motioned to the woods. "I found animal tracks—most likely deer."

"*Ach,*" she said, frustration coloring

the one word. "I've been so distracted, I haven't had time to check down here. Deer do love daylilies."

"You mentioned this could happen," he said, staring down at the trampled, half-eaten plants. "But I didn't know to check here."

"It's not your fault, Jeb. I need to put up a fence or use some kind of deterrent, but I need money and time to do that."

She placed her hands on her hips, wondering what could happen next.

"I'll handle it," he said. "I can build a sturdy fence."

"But we can't fence the whole field."

He looked from the front of the field to the back, where the Green Mountain hills sat against the horizon. "No. We will take it one row at a time, if need be."

"That will take a long time, Jeb."

He stopped and stared over at her, realization making him frown. "Rebecca..."

"Don't," she said. "I know you might not be here forever, but for now, *ja*, I need some sort of fence. We'll clear this up and then I'll sit down and go over the budget."

She turned and hurried toward the house before he could tell her the truth. He had obviously decided to leave soon. Maybe sooner than he'd planned. She wished she'd never let him kiss her. And she wished she'd never kissed him back.

Jeb went into town and bought as much fence wire as he could find, then he loaded some fence posts onto the hauling buggy. He wouldn't have much time to work on the shed project. This new fence would take up most of the week and next week.

Mr. Hartford came out the back door of the general store. "Jeb, you got another project going on?"

"*Ja*. I'm going to try and fence up the back part of Becca's lily field—the section closest to the woods. The deer have found it."

"I see," Mr. Hartford said. "You'll need

some help with that. It'll have to be a mighty tall fence to keep deer out."

"I can do it," Jeb replied, hoping that he wouldn't be proved wrong. "I'm buying tall posts and I'm going to wire it tight and high."

"All you have to do is put out the word," Mr. Hartford said. "You know your neighbors will show up."

Jeb finished loading the fence posts. "You are correct," he said with a grin. "I tend to forget that."

"Well, I hear you're back for good," the storeowner said. "Make the most of it and don't break your back. Then you won't be able to help anyone." After looking around, he added, "The Amish like to be helpful and since you're new around here, you'll become more endeared to them if you don't shun that help."

Jeb laughed and turned to his friend. "I'll do that. Thanks for the reminder. If I get a few able bodies, I can get this done much faster."

"Then you can return to your secret project," Mr. Hartford said with a wink. "And besides, anyone around here would want to help Rebecca. She's one of the kindest people I know."

"I cannot argue with that," Jeb said, wishing he could shout it to the rooftops. But other than anything work related, Rebecca had been avoiding him. She must have decided that kiss was a bad idea. Or... Noah had said something to her about Jeb being related to John.

Jeb left and headed home. He'd get the word out that Becca needed help. Her good name would bring people, but his hard work could get the back fence in place. The deer would have to take a long detour if they wanted to nibble more lilies.

By the time he'd made it home, he had enough men to help. He'd first stopped at Micah's house. Micah had readily agreed.

Then Micah told him he'd help get the word out.

Noah showed up just as Jeb was unloading the fence posts.

"I heard Becca had deer trouble, and I'm not referring to you."

"Funny," Jeb said. Then he explained what he planned.

Noah listened, nodding. "I told her last time this happened I'd get her a fence up, but I got busy and neglected that. So, I'm here to help today."

Soon, buggies pulled up with more posts and fence wire.

Jeb saw Rebecca hurrying out of the house, her expression full of surprise. "What is all this?"

Noah chuckled. "Your worker here is going to fence up the back side of the property, to hopefully keep the deer away. Word got out that he might need some help."

Rebecca glanced from her bemused brother back to Jeb. "Is this true?" She looked out over the field and then back.

"That would mean from the road to the creek."

"*Ja,*" he said, wondering if she'd get mad. "Now I can fence up almost half of the open field, and after we save up a bit more, I can finish fencing the whole field, almost up to the creek. I'll put a fence there with a gate but leave room to walk along the creek. Mr. Hartford suggested I find some help to get this first phase going, and, well, word got around pretty quickly."

"I can see how the word spread," she replied. "I'm amazed that you thought of everything—even leaving the creek walking trail open. You sure make a good assistant, Jeb. I'm not sure what I'll do when you're gone."

Then she turned to head to the house.

Jeb glanced at Noah. "Does that mean she approves or that she's mad?"

Noah shook his head. "I can't figure women, but I think she's grateful, and if I know my sister, she's getting a pitcher of water or lemonade for us and probably finding some snacks, too."

"You could be right," Jeb replied, still worried. "I haven't had a chance to talk to her, Noah."

Noah gave him a disappointed stare. "I can tell you've been busy. But soon, Jeb. Better make it soon because Shem is a *gut* man and a *gut* friend, but he likes to stick his nose in everyone's business. Wouldn't you rather she hears this from you than from someone else?"

Jeb nodded, but the others were gathering, ready to work. "I promise, I'll tell her the truth, Noah. You have my word on that."

Noah gave him a slight nod. "Let's see what we can get done on this fence today. But I'll hold you to that promise."

Hannah showed up to help.

"How did you know?" Rebecca asked her sister when she met Hannah at the door to help her carry in some food.

"How does anyone know anything around here?" Hannah asked, laughing. "That grapevine keeps growing."

"*Denke* for coming over."

Hannah hugged her. "Of course. I brought some sandwiches and chips. Samuel will *kumm* later when he gets home from work."

Rebecca glanced out the back window. "I can't believe this is happening. I have to fight off deer every season."

"That's because you never asked for help," her sister said with a shrug. "Apparently, Jeb didn't either. But Mr. Hartford gave him a nudge since you never listen to his advice."

"I always thought Mr. Hartford was being kind, and felt sorry for me because I'm all alone," she admitted.

Hannah made a face. "No one feels sorry for you. You're an established businesswoman and your business brings in tourists and locals alike. That benefits all of the companies around here, Becca. You need to see your own value to this community."

Rebecca sat down, shocked. "I've never thought of it that way. Mr. Hartford knows if I succeed and have an easier way of doing things, I'll benefit him and the entire town."

"You can't see the good you do," Hannah replied, her tone gentle. "But we can, and Jeb surely can. He's already improved things around here."

"He has done so much," she admitted. "But I still don't know if I can count on him to stay."

"He's doing everything he can to settle down, from what I hear," Hannah replied. "Everyone's talking about him getting ready to commit to his faith again. Why can't you believe that?"

Rebecca stood and went back to work. "I want to believe he means to stay, but I don't want to get my hopes up. Things can change in the blink of an eye."

She couldn't bring herself to tell Hannah that she and Jeb circled around each other—sometimes talking and laughing, other times avoiding each other. They'd done that since that one kiss.

She didn't plan on sharing that information either. If Noah got word of that—he'd set the wedding date for certain sure.

Hannah came to stand by her. "I know you'll never get over losing John, but you can't base every decision on what might go wrong. Try trusting *Gott* and yourself, for a change. Try focusing on what could go right. And try focusing on Jeb doing the right thing instead of wondering when he might walk away."

"Are you through?" she asked her sister with a teasing smile.

"*Neh*, I'm just getting started," Hannah shot back. "You're too stubborn for your own good at times."

Rebecca nodded. "I suppose I am at that. I won't forget what Jeb—and all of you— are doing for me. I'll ask for help from now on. If I need it."

"We all need it," Hannah said. "Now, let's get this food in place out on the porch. You know those men will be hungry once they finish this task."

Rebecca gathered trays and drink cups. "What a *wunderbar* thing—no more deer, or maybe even no Old Billy breaking out to sample my lilies."

"And a new understanding about yourself," her sister added.

"I'm not sure how you became so wise," she told Hannah, "but I love you for it."

"I love you, too," Hannah said. "And I like that light that sparkles in your eyes when you're looking at Jeb."

"I do not have a light or a sparkle," she retorted. "Jeb and I are friends. He's a *gut* worker."

Hannah snickered. "Just keep telling yourself that."

"I will."

They both giggled like teenagers, making Rebecca remember the days when they were young.

"I miss Mamm and Daed," she said. "I could use their wisdom these days."

"They are always with us," Hannah reminded her. "They taught us well."

"*Ja*, they did at that."

Rebecca watched as Jeb and the other men dug holes and stretched fence wire. While she appreciated the help, she also realized she needed someone around here to help her all the time.

She needed Jeb, in more ways than just for work.

But she'd keep that secret to herself for now.

Chapter Seventeen

Two days later, the weather turned nasty. Thunderstorms shook the earth with lightning, and rain fell in heavy silver sheets of mist. Jeb had to shut down the fencing, but with the help of most of the men in the community, they'd managed to complete the high fence directly next to the woods. The deer gathered there most nights, so the fence had become a way to hinder them from eating the lilies. But he needed to get the rest of the fence up, and soon.

"Your fence helps with so many issues," Rebecca told him as they sat on the porch that afternoon, waiting for the rain to lift.

"Now if we could find a way to keep the *kinder* from crashing through the rows, too. They are like little lambs after the pretty blooms."

He laughed at that image. Children running through the fields. Somehow, that made his heart ache more than it made him mad. "You're right, there. Children are less inhibited than adults."

She glanced over at him. "Are you thinking about your brother?"

He nodded. "I guess I was. Pauly stayed childlike...up until he died at thirteen. Everything was a joy to him. Everything but our *daed*."

Shock darkened her eyes. "I can't imagine how that must have been. My parents were so gentle, so kind. I'd like to think I'd be the same if I ever had a child."

"You'd make a great mother, Becca."

She lifted her head, her gaze on him. "You did the best you could with Pauly, I'm sure."

Jeb stared out as the wind picked up and

the trees swayed. "I tried, but I wasn't always patient with him."

He closed his eyes and asked God to help him. Then he looked over at Rebecca. "I'm the reason he's dead."

"What?" Yet another jolt of shock—because of him telling her the truth. But Jeb felt he had to tell her something about his past. Maybe he'd get up the nerve to tell her about John's letters, too.

"He'd run away when Daed got really mean, usually to where I worked in a buggy repair shop."

"What happened?" Rebecca said. "I won't judge you, Jeb. You've been punishing yourself enough for the both of us."

She saw so many things not spoken, he thought. "*Ja*, I have at that."

"Then let go of some of your pain. Tell me and it will stay here between us."

Jeb stared at his glass of tea. "I was busy when he came running in, crying. When Pauly got in that kind of frantic mood, he was hard to contain." He stopped, gathered his emotions. But the lump in his throat wouldn't go away. "He was crying and stomping. My boss had been kind about these episodes, but on that day, we had some important visitors from a furniture place in Pittsburgh. They were interested in having us do a huge order for wardrobes and rocking chairs."

"You needed to focus on work, and your upset *bruder* showed up?"

He nodded. "My boss wasn't happy. It was the worst possible time for Pauly to have a meltdown."

"What happened?"

"I excused myself and took him out back. I tried to get him to settle down and wait there at the picnic table. I promised I'd get him a hamburger—his favorite food."

Rebecca smiled at that. "I like hamburgers myself." Then she nudged Jeb. "Go on."

"I left him there, fuming and crying. He kept repeating, 'I don't like Daed. I don't like Daed.'" Jeb swallowed again, his heart burning with sorrow and guilt. "I hurried back inside to finish up with our customers and when I finally went back out, Pauly was gone."

Rebecca put a hand to her lips. "Oh, no."

Jeb studied her, looking for condemnation. When he saw none, he decided he needed to tell her the rest of the story. "I went searching for him along the roadside. After a few minutes, I spotted him up the way and ran toward him, calling to him."

Rebecca put a hand on his arm, her eyes meeting his.

"When he saw me, he ran toward me." Jeb gulped in air, his heart hammering. "But he didn't look both ways, Becca. He didn't look. He only wanted his brother. The pickup truck never saw him coming. It all happened in a few seconds and then... He was gone."

Rebecca stood and then kneeled in front of Jeb, her hands grasping his. "This is not your fault, Jeb. Pauly was a special child and *Gott* knew that."

He lifted away and stood. "Then why did *Gott* let that happen to him? He was upset and he was innocent. Pauly didn't care if I had work to do. He needed me and I failed him."

Rebecca was there by him, the rain and wind slashing at their clothes, water falling off the eaves to wet them. She turned Jeb to face her, then she put a hand on his jaw. "Jeb, you did not cause this. It was a tragic accident, a horrible accident. You have to see that."

Jeb looked into her misty eyes and shook his head. "What I see every day and every night is my Pauly flying through the air and then landing on the asphalt road. Then he didn't move. He never moved. He never woke up."

"Jeb," she whispered. "Jeb." Then she tugged him into her arms and held him. "I'm here. *Gott* is here. You've found a home now, and you can seek forgiveness and comfort."

Jeb's emotions exploded with as much fire as the pounding rain. The wind washed at his tears while Rebecca held him and hugged him. He sobbed until he had no tears left.

But Rebecca didn't move. She didn't walk away. She didn't ask him to leave her property. Instead, she stayed with him.

Finally, he lifted his head and wiped at his eyes. "Rebecca?"

"*Ja?*"

"You are an amazing woman."

Her bashful expression showed she didn't believe that.

"I mean it," he said. "I've never told anyone about this—about my part in this. Daed, of course, blamed me and acted as if he really cared. After the way he'd treated Pauly, his reaction made me angry, and we had words—horrible words said to each other. Once I'd buried my brother next to my *mamm*, I left Ohio. I've been searching for something since then."

"You were searching for redemption, Jeb. And now you've found it."

Jeb saw by her earnest expression that she meant those words. He held her, their eyes meeting, and with a sigh Rebecca lifted up and pressed her lips on his. The kiss was soft and welcoming and full of that redemption he'd needed for so long.

When she pulled away, she studied his face and gave him a soft smile. "How do you feel now?"

Jeb touched her wet hair, one finger tracing a loose curl. "I feel as if I've been washed clean. I feel...hopeful." He was about to tell her the rest—about John.

But a clap of lightning filled the sky, and the world went dark.

Becca automatically tugged him close, more from fright than anything else. Then they both stepped back and checked the clouds.

"This weather is about to get worse," he said. "Let's get inside."

Grabbing her hand, Jeb rushed Rebecca into the house and shut the door. The trees leaned sideways as walls of water and wind pushed over the land and lashed at the earth. Small limbs twisted from the trees and catapulted across the yard.

"My lilies," she said, her voice hollow with fear. "This could ruin my whole crop."

Jeb tugged her away from the window. "Let's pray that won't happen."

They sat on the stairs, holding tight to each other while the world outside screamed and thundered with a mighty rage.

Jeb could understand that kind of rage, but while the storm hissed and sneered, he managed to let go of some of his own rage. And he had Rebecca—and God—to thank for that.

After the storm ended, leaving a soft drizzle behind, they put on muck boots and rain capes and went to check on the crops. Sure enough, Rebecca found some damaged stems.

"If the blooms are broken past about two-thirds of the stem, that plant might not produce again. I need to check on the cutting plants. Remember when I explained I have customers who want to have fresh-cut lilies in their homes. They come back each year to buy more just for cutting and displays, so those plants are considered annuals. Those might be damaged the worst since they're near a low spot that rushes with water in storms like this one. They won't like being too soggy either. That causes the bulbs to rot."

"Remind me the spot and I'll go check those," Jeb said, a new reassurance between them now.

She pointed to a corner near the barn. "I'll be there in a moment or two. I want to check my more-expensive plants, the ones people like to grow for shows. I have some beautiful Casablanca lilies that should bloom later in the year if they didn't get too damaged."

They parted, her going toward the best of her hybrids, and Jeb rushing toward the plot of lilies growing near the barn and the rushing creek.

Lily Dog came running from the barn, her yelps showing she didn't like storms either. The shaggy little mutt shivered in the cool air as she trotted along with Rebecca.

"It's okay," Rebecca said, bending to pat the wet dog on the head. "Just a big blow over, is all."

Rebecca hurried through the showstoppers, as she liked to call them. She got top dollar for these cultivars. She'd lose a chunk of her profits if they'd been damaged. Such was the way of any farmer. The crops depended on the weather, but the weather could turn on the crops. Nature was always something awesome, and it required a lot of respect.

After walking the rows, she found a few

spots where the early blooms had been snapped off, and several plants that had been bruised or crushed by the heavy wind and rain. Some of the taller stems had broken, so she would have that to deal with.

Finally, she emerged and looked toward where Jeb stood near the other plants. Lily Dog woofed and took off toward Jeb. Rebecca followed, too tired to hurry.

"These look bad," he said, nodding toward the short rows of lush plants. "Most are damaged or broken."

"We'll replant and hope for the best," she said. "It could have been a lot worse. We'll clean up, prune and get things going again."

"How can you be so calm?" Jeb asked, his eyes on her now.

"I'm used to this," she replied. "One year I had aphids so bad, I lost half my crop. Another, a tornado flattened everything in Campton Creek, and that's how Micah met Samantha, or Leah, as we all call her. The tornado lifted her car and it landed in his wheat field. She has a little dog named Patch—reminds me of our Lily Dog."

"I've got a lot of catching up to do," Jeb said with a grin. The dog barked in agreement.

"*Kumm* inside," she said, her voice hollow and tired. "I'll fix us some *kaffe* and we'll make a quick dinner."

"Are you sure?" he asked, his gaze still on her.

Rebecca took his hand. "I'm sure, Jeb. You've done so much for me. I owe you more than I can say."

"What if I want more than gratitude?" he asked.

Rebecca's finger tightened over his. "We have all summer," she said. "Let's see how we feel when fall arrives."

Jeb squeezed her hand back. "I hope fall takes its dear sweet time getting here."

Chapter Eighteen

Jeb had the damaged part of the garden replanted and reworked in a few days. He suggested they build up the soil there to keep that patch of lilies from being flooded with water after each rain. This project had kept him busy, and it had given him time to think hard on what he should do next. He'd shared the worst part of his past, and Rebecca had kissed him during the storm. His heart filled with joy in that moment, but he had tried since to avoid her as much as possible. He wouldn't let this go any further with his one last secret standing between them. It wouldn't be fair to her.

But he sure did like being with her, helping her, making her livelihood stronger and more secure. And he could tell she was beginning to feel the same. Would she forgive him after he told her the truth?

He prayed so and hoped to find the right time to come clean. It had been a few days since the storm, so he'd had limbs to clear away and lilies to pamper. They'd both been hard at work. Rebecca's garden was overflowing, so she'd been over at Franny's house most of the week, canning and freezing vegetables and making fruit preserves.

The day was coming to an end. He'd have to stop and go take care of the animals.

Now, he stood back and checked the new grid. He'd moved wheelbarrows of soil from the outskirts of the fields to this area, building it up until he'd managed to level it off. Then he'd made a dirt drain full of rocks beside the grid, so any rainwater should flow away from the lilies planted there. It looked different, but clean and ready to go. He'd taken the bulbs with stems Rebecca said they could transplant from the big garden and planted them deep into the soil. Rebecca said they should start producing in a few weeks.

"I see this project is done," Noah said as he strolled toward Jeb. "That's a much better layout than the original. This part of the garden was an afterthought that turned into a new responsibility for Becca."

"Well, now it's my responsibility," Jeb said, wondering what Noah was doing here so late in the day.

"You are taking on a lot more of the everyday tasks," Noah replied, holding his suspenders.

"What's wrong?" Jeb finally asked, his instincts telling him he probably did know why Noah was here.

Noah looked him over. "You haven't told her yet, have you?"

"No," Jeb said, since he had no excuse except hard work and a deep dread holding him back. "I took some time earlier in the week to tell Bishop King and he agrees she should know. He thinks she'll appreciate my being kin to John once the dust settles."

"If the dust settles," Noah replied. "The longer you wait, the harder it will become."

Jeb nodded. "I know. But I'm finishing up her garden shed. I have all the boards marked so all we have to do is haul them to the spot I've measured and get going on putting the whole thing together. Are you still willing to help?"

"Are you still willing to be honest with her?" Noah shot back.

"I will tell her everything," Jeb replied, "after her birthday and after she sees the shed."

"And then what?"

"And then I'll either be a forgiven man, and I can stay. Or I'll be in a bad spot again, and I'll leave." He stopped, took in a breath. "As a heartbroken man. Still."

Noah shook his head. "I can't be the one to tell her. And I cautioned Shem on passing what he'd figured out to anyone because he wasn't for certain sure, but we don't want Shem messing around and letting it slip if he runs into Rebecca."

"I know." Jeb took off his straw hat and swept a hand through his hair. "I know. I've made a mess of things, but, Noah, Becca and I are growing close. There will come the Sunday I'll go before the church and confess all."

"Even this last secret."

"Even that, but I want her to know before that happens."

"So do I," Noah replied. "She'd be mighty upset to hear this with all the brethren around her. She'd be humiliated."

Jeb didn't want that to happen. "I could go and talk to Shem. Would you go with me?"

"And aid you in keeping this a secret?"

Noah asked. "I'm already doing that. I won't keep adding to the lie."

"It's not a lie. I'm only trying to protect your sister."

"Neh," Noah said. "You're only protecting yourself and that's the worst thing you can do at this point."

After Noah left, Jeb stood staring at the creek. Noah was right. He needed to get this one last hurdle out of the way and then he could truly feel free and clear—cleansed and complete. He had run out of excuses.

He prayed Rebecca's gracious heart and her promise of not judging him would still hold when he told her the truth.

"Noah, have you said something to Jeb again—about me?"

Rebecca knew something was wrong. She'd sensed a change in Jeb now that they were back to their routines and clearing away the storm damage. He and Adam stayed busy, of course. But Adam followed him into the barn in the late afternoon and then they walked home together. No more suppers alone with Jeb.

He'd kissed her there on the porch the other night, with the rain falling all around them. Rather, she'd kissed him. Why had she gone and done that? Now he'd shut down again and managed to avoid her at every turn. He stayed in the barn until late in the day, after they'd done their chores. Was he ashamed that he'd told her what had happened to Pauly? Or had her brother somehow seen them and told him to stop kissing Rebecca?

"Noah?"

Noah frowned, then he looked away. Then he frowned again. "What do you mean?"

"I mean, he is barely talking to me and after work, he heads to either my barn or yours. How many harnesses can a man mend?"

Noah almost smiled, then he shook his head. "I think, sister, Jeb is at a crossroads.

He likes it here and he aims to stay, but whatever he's been through is causing him to doubt. He's afraid he'll be hurt again. Heartbroken even."

"Then you have been talking to him!" Had Jeb told her brother all that he'd shared with her about his past, his *daed* and Pauly?

Flustered, Noah tugged at his beard, a sure sign he had something on his mind. "We talk, *ja*. He's around a lot, so I talk to him. Surely you aren't upset about that. I thought you wanted me to be nice to him."

Rebecca started walking with Noah toward her house. She'd come over to visit with Katie and Franny and to help process some of the first crops of wild blueberries and blackberries, and the fresh vegetables from both of their thriving gardens.

Today, they'd blanched beans and peas, and shucked and cleaned fresh corn to store in the propane-operated refrigerator. Noah was helping her carry her baskets full of jars of jam and vegetables back home to put in the storage room in the basement.

"I do want you to be nice to him," she said. "I don't want you pestering him or pushing him off on me."

Noah's thick eyebrows lifted like a set of wings. "Well, I thought you were beginning to like him, same as me."

She had to be careful what she told her brother. He'd get the wrong impression and meddle even more. "I do care about Jeb. He's one of us and he's been fighting a hard battle. He and I get along, but he's been acting strange lately. Not as friendly and talkative. Now I think I understand. He's still struggling, ain't so?"

"Struggling how?" Noah asked, surprised.

"You just said it yourself. He's reached a time of no return. He either comes back to the Amish life, or he has to move on. Is that what you've talked about?"

Her brother looked both ways when they reached the narrow ribbon of road. "*Ja,* sure. We've talked about that and a lot of things."

"So... This is why he's been so distant? He's still having doubts even though he says he's going to be okay?"

"*Ja*, that could be it."

Frustrated, Rebecca shifted her basket of blueberry preserves. Noah answered her in riddles. He was either protecting her, or he was protecting Jeb. Maybe both of them.

"Well, thank you for making all this as clear as mud."

Noah carried the jars of beans and crushed tomatoes into the kitchen. "So now you're cross with me?"

"I'm not cross with anyone," she said. After placing her basket on the table, she turned to Noah. "I'm having doubts, too. I don't know how I feel about Jeb or anything else these days."

Noah's eyes widened, and he twitched like a newborn foal. "Has he done or said something to hurt you?"

"*Neh,* I'm fine. He's respectful in every

way, he works hard, and your little chaperone hangs on his every word."

She hoped she wasn't blushing, but each time she thought of their kisses, she got all warm and dreamy. Her brother didn't need to know that. "I'm just used to having Moses Yoder following me around. He rarely talked, mostly grunted and nodded and mumbled."

Her brother grinned. "Jeb is quite different from Old Moses."

"*Ja*, and there's the problem. He is my friend, and he works for me. It's a lot different."

Concern rimmed Noah's face, causing her even more worry. "In a good way, or a bad way?"

Her brother's genuine sincerity touched Rebecca. "That's the confusing part. In a good way, and in a bad way. Jeb is a *gut* man and he's doing all he can to come back to his faith. But just like Jeb, I don't want to ever be heartbroken again either." Then she put her hands on her hips.

"Which is why you need to stop playing matchmaker to us."

Noah nodded, his fingers moving down his beard. "And that means I must not worry about the both of you being here alone with each other so much. I miss Old Moses, for certain sure."

Rebecca patted her brother on the arm. "Noah, you do not need to worry on my account. I'm grown now, remember?"

"Every day, I remember this," he said. "I dread when Katie grows up and starts walking out with boys. I will not like it, not one bit."

"But you won't be able to hold her back either," Rebecca said. "I can figure out my life, and you go and take care of your *wunderbar* family. If I have doubts, I promise I will *kumm* to you. You are so much like our *daed*."

Noah's eyes misted. "I will take that as a compliment."

"You have been *gut* to me and you've

watched over me for a long time. I know I can depend on you."

"Even when I overstep?"

"Even so," she said with a smile.

Noah looked uncertain, making her suspicious all over again. But she knew him well enough to think she wouldn't get any information out of him unless he wanted her to know it.

"Now, go," she told him. "I'm tired and it's almost suppertime."

Noah nodded. Then he turned at the door. "I won't force you and Jeb together. I think this is something you two have to decide on your own, with prayer and consideration. If *Gott* wants you together, it will work itself out."

"*Denke,*" Rebecca said. "I'm glad you've come to that conclusion."

Noah nodded, started to speak and then shook his head. With a sigh, he turned. "I'll see you later, then."

Rebecca watched her brother go, still not sure. Something was up. Noah knew

more than he was letting on. She'd never
seen her brother so befuddled or *verhud-
delt*—confused. Noah always spoke his
mind, and especially about Jeb. But he'd
hesitated today.

She had to wonder what her brother and
Jeb were hiding from her.

Jeb finished the fence, doing most of the
last bits of work after he'd completed his
other chores. Adam helped, talking away
about fishing, riding his bike, milking
cows and goats, and just about any subject.
Jeb let the boy talk, and he answered when
asked a question. That gave him time to
his own thoughts, mostly about Rebecca
and how much he appreciated this job.

"Hey, Jeb?"

He looked up to find Adam holding a
hammer. *"Ja?"*

Adam scrunched his nose. "Are you mad
at me?"

Jeb stopped tugging at the leftover fencing wire and turned to the boy. "What makes you think I'm mad at you?"

Adam put his hammer on the fence post next to him. "You ain't been talking much lately, is all."

Jeb had so much on his mind, he'd shut down a bit. His young helper must have picked up on that. "Well, I'm letting you do most of the talking. You entertain me and that keeps me from wanting to take a nap."

Adam grinned at that. "My *mamm* says my talking puts her to sleep."

"Well, it keeps me awake," Jeb replied, thinking the boy might splutter along, but he was observant. "I do have a lot going on—things I have to fret about."

"So you're not mad, you're just stewing in your head?"

"Exactly. Stewing a lot."

"You're gonna stay here, right?"

Jeb took a sip of the big water jug Rebecca always provided. "I haven't decided, but I'm ninety percent sure that I will be staying past summer."

"I'm glad," Adam said. "You're like one of my best friends. I want you to be one hundred percent for certain sure."

Jeb was so touched, he had to blink and look away. He prayed for 100 percent. "I'm glad we're friends," he said, his voice husky because of the big lump stuck in his throat. "You know, I had a brother who followed me around all the time."

Adam's eyes got big with surprise. "You did? I didn't know that." Then his expression changed, and he hung his head. "You said once you'd lost two people you loved. Was your *bruder* one of them?"

"Ja," Jeb said, his heart burning. "My *mamm* died when I was a teenager. My *daed* wasn't an easy man to live with, so I tried to take care of Pauly—my brother. I didn't do such a good job."

"Well, most kids need a *mamm*, ain't so?"

"You are right there, my friend. Pauly and I sure needed our *mamm*."

Adam stared over at him. "I'd be sad if my *mamm* passed. Is that why you don't tell about it much? Cause it might make you cry?"

Jeb loved this kid. "I don't talk about it much because it still hurts and because I've made a lot of mistakes in my time of grief. Pauly died when he was a bit older than you."

Adam leaned over the nearest fence post. "That's a shame. Terrible. My *bruders* get on my last nerve sometimes, but I'd be sad if something happened to either of 'em."

"It does make me sad," Jeb admitted. "I've been angry about it, so sometimes I get quiet and...moody. But you need to know I'd never be mad at you. You're right—we're best friends."

Adam's grin made all the bad thoughts go away. Jeb had to wonder what it would be like to have a son like Adam, so inquisitive, so full of life and promise.

Then he thought about Rebecca, could see her holding a baby. If they were to marry, could they have a child? Or had they already missed that time in their lives?

He didn't dare dream any further. There was still a lot he needed to work through before he could even contemplate marriage and a family. But he already knew in his heart, he wanted to be with Rebecca, children or no children.

Chapter Nineteen

❧

"You have a birthday soon."

Rebecca glanced at her sister. Hannah always showed up on Saturday to lend her a hand or help her with customers. Now that she had Jeb and Adam, Rebecca had more time to keep things organized. This morning, she and Hannah were watching over the gardens while Jeb and Adam sold plants and produce up on the road.

They'd pulled two lawn chairs out into the shade of the old oak near the field, with a small wooden table between them serving as Rebecca's desk. Rebecca let her customers roam on their own until they needed her help. Hannah had made a huge container of honey lemonade to offer their visitors, and she'd brought paper cups to serve the sweet, refreshing drink. Rebecca handed out the pamphlets Jeb and Jewel had created, so customers could read her tips and pass that information on to others. That one gesture had brought her a lot more business.

"I'm trying to forget my birthday," she told her sister while she kept her eyes on the half-dozen people milling around her gardens. The fields were at their prime, so she expected a lot of business today. "I'm getting older by the minute."

"You still look young. Mamm always looked so young. You take after her." Then Hannah shrugged. "The *Englisch* don't think being in your thirties is old, you know."

"The *Englisch* are different from us, you know," Rebecca shot back with a smile.

"*Ja*, they just have fancy doctors to lift everything," Hannah said with a giggle.

"Hannah!" Rebecca never knew what would come out of her sister's mouth. But Hannah did make a valid point. "I'm past worrying about wrinkles and such. I'm thankful I've made it this far."

"You and Jeb are about the same age."

"Really, I hadn't noticed," she quipped. Did everyone around here want her to marry Jeb?

"Have you thought about him anymore?"

Rebecca wanted to say she thought about nothing else, but she wouldn't give anyone fodder or hope. "I work with him, so *ja*, I think about him a lot when I'm planning out the daily tasks around here."

"That's not what I meant."

Rebecca gave her sister a frown. "I know what you meant, and I have no answers. I care about Jeb. We've grown close, but that information is between you and me. Noah has backed off, at least. He knows I like Jeb and that's all he needs to know."

"So if you and Jeb were to become really close, it won't be because our brother demanded it, ain't so?"

"That is correct. It will happen naturally and because it is the Lord's plan for our lives." Rebecca watched her customers and then she turned back to Hannah. "Have you heard Noah talking about Jeb? Our brother seemed skittish the other day when he came by to talk."

Hannah shook her head. "Noah doesn't confide in me. He thinks I can't keep a secret."

Rebecca raised her eyebrows and they both started laughing.

"Okay, so maybe I do find it hard to not repeat things," Hannah said, "but Noah won't tell me any gossip, so I can't repeat what I don't know."

"Noah likes Jeb now, same as me. I'm beginning to think those two are in cahoots about something."

"You know how men are—they hold everything in, trying to be all manly. Maybe

Jeb shared something with Noah that he didn't want to talk about with anyone else."

Rebecca stood, her mind reeling with possibilities. "That is the best answer anyone could give me. Men do talk, but they speak differently than women."

"*Ja*, and we are all thankful for that," Hannah replied.

"So, if Noah and Jeb have been talking and passing secrets, that means our brother trusts Jeb, at least."

"And that also means Jeb must hold trust in our stubborn, well-meaning brother," Hannah said, proud of herself.

"This could be *gut*," Rebecca replied, relief washing over her. "Whatever those two have going on, I will stay out of it. Just to keep the peace around here."

A customer approached with a question, so she hurried off to help. Hannah poured more lemonade and then went to help another customer. Soon Rebecca got so busy, she didn't worry overmuch about how strange her brother had been acting.

But if Noah and Jeb were growing closer, why did Jeb seem to be avoiding her at every turn? Noah might have befriended Jeb, but he might also still be trying to push Jeb toward her.

Would she ever understand how Jeb really felt about her?

He'd tried.

Jeb let out a sigh as the last of the marked timber was put away. He could finally build the potting shed he'd imagined for Rebecca. Meantime, he'd tried every which way to find the courage to tell her about John. Her John, his cousin. He had letters written by the man she'd loved.

Why can't I just be honest with her?

He finished up in the barn, hiding the last of the wood he'd managed to saw and shape into a passable puzzle that had to be put together in a few hours while she was away.

Noah was in charge of making that happen. He'd explained to Franny that she should invite Hannah and Rebecca for a town day. They'd buy fabric for dresses and quilting, thread, anything they needed to make Franny's soap and candles and anything that could keep them away for a few hours. Next Saturday afternoon, after they'd done their half day of work.

Franny would use Rebecca's birthday as an excuse to get her away from the house. It just happened to fall on a Saturday this year.

Noah had given him a grace period.

"You don't want to upset her before or on her birthday. So get this done and then, Jeb, you have to be honest with her. Or I'll have to be the one to tell her, and that will make it twice as humiliating for her."

Jeb's head hurt from lack of sleep, trying to keep a secret surprise, and having a bombshell secret he'd kept from Rebecca.

"You look sad."

Surprised, he found Franny standing in the barn door with a glass heavy with sliced lemons and tea.

"I have a lot on my mind," he admitted. Noah's wife was quiet and steady, like the creek behind Rebecca's house. She didn't gossip and she kept her four children under control. But she rarely talked to Jeb. "Did you need something?"

She offered him the drink. "I need to speak to you."

Jeb got that feeling of dread in his stomach. "All right." He took a sip of lemony-sweet tea with mint. "This is *gut*."

"I'm trying new versions," Franny admitted. "I read about mixing tea and lemonade in a magazine at the doctor's office. Sounded refreshing, *ja*?"

"It is that."

Franny's shy smile changed to seriousness. "I know what you have planned for Rebecca. I think this is truly kind of you, Jeb. She will be so touched."

"I hope so. I want to make her life easier."

Franny nodded. "I wanted to apologize for judging you when you first showed up here. I've heard nothing but the best about you from day one. Most of that coming from Adam, of course. He really looks up to you."

"Adam is a *gut* kid, and we're best friends."

"He has learned a lot from you," Franny said, smiling. "Noah is so busy, and he tries to take time with all the boys, so letting Adam work with you has also helped him become closer to his *daed*, too."

"How's that?" Jeb asked, wishing he could have discovered some way to help his *daed* and Pauly become closer.

"Adam is a talker, inquisitive and smart. Noah doesn't often have the patience to deal with that. But now that Adam has been around you, he has also learned to speak to Noah in a different way, with understanding and respect. I owe you for that, Jeb."

Jeb's heart swelled with pride for Adam. Not for himself. "It's easy being around

Adam. We've had some great conversations."

"Maybe I should send the other two over to take lessons from you, *ja*?"

He laughed, afraid Franny might be serious. When she grinned, he breathed a sigh of relief. "You had me there for a minute."

She laughed again. Then she said, "Don't worry. I'll get Hannah and Rebecca away so you can build the shed. Hannah only knows I want to take them into town to celebrate a bit. As you know, we don't go all out for birthdays. But I can't wait to see Becca's reaction when she comes home to find it there."

"Let's hope she'll be pleased."

Franny gave him a knowing smile. "She will be pleased because you are a thoughtful person, someone she admires."

"*Denke*, Franny," he said, handing her back the almost empty glass. "I hope she'll like the new shed."

Franny left, and Jeb stood there taking in a breath. He'd won over so many doubters. But how could he win over the one person he wanted to believe in him and trust him? How could he win over Rebecca after being dishonest with her for weeks now?

One more week until her birthday and the shed being built. Could he wait another week? He had no choice. He wouldn't mess up her surprise. If she told him to leave later, at least she'd have that gift to use and maybe to remember he did have a good, caring side to him. He wanted her to remember the good in him, not his one sin of omission.

The days seemed to flow for Rebecca. She kept thinking about her birthday. She'd long ago given up on a husband and children, letting her niece and nephews give her the joy of what must feel like mothering her own child. But each time she glanced at Jeb, she wished she could be ten years younger.

Silly, but he'd make a great father.

That could be the thing between them that no one talked about—that she might be too old to have children. Did he think about that? Just one more reason for them to remain friends.

He'd been a bit more talkative lately, but she felt as if they were walking a fine line. So she decided to take matters into her own hands. She'd learned long ago if you want something done, do it yourself.

"Jeb," she said late on a Thursday after they'd had a busy day in the heat of summer, "I'd like you to stay for supper tonight."

Jeb had been gathering vegetables, as he liked to do at the end of the day. The asparagus and cabbage were both exploding, so they had to constantly gather buckets full of both. She and Franny would make sauerkraut with the cabbage, and they could eat the asparagus fresh and sell most of it. He glanced up in surprise, his cutting scissors in one hand. "Are you sure?"

"I wouldn't ask if I weren't sure," she retorted, the sting of his words hitting their mark. "Unless you have other plans."

"My only plan is to wash up, find food and collapse," he admitted. "I've cut a whole row of cabbage and cleared off the outside leaves. And this asparagus is ready to clip so I want to finish this row."

"*Denke* for doing that, but if you're tired, you might not want to linger or eat a real meal."

"I didn't say that."

She took one of the buckets and started clearing heavy green cabbage leaves from the sturdy stems. "Why are you avoiding me, Jeb? Is it because I was bold enough to kiss you? Did that make you think less of me?"

Jeb put his bucket down and stared at her. "Kissing you would never make me think less of you, Becca. It only made me want to kiss you more."

She blushed but blamed the heat rising up her face on the warm day. "I see."

"*Neh*, that is the problem," he said, his

brow wet with sweat. "You do not see. You fight against what we are feeling because you are just as afraid as I am, aren't you?"

She set her bucket down with a thud. "What do I have to fear, Jeb?"

"Everything," he said, frustration echoing out behind that one word. "I'm a stranger. I need to confess everything to become Amish again. I'm a hard man to deal with, a man who has a past. That's a lot to have to accept."

"I have accepted you in every way," she replied, anger and frustration boiling over. "Is there anything else I need to know? Is it me? Because I'm old and I can't bear children? Is it because everyone wants you to marry me, so they can all stop feeling sorry for me?"

"Becca…" He started for her, but Lily Dog chose that moment to come running toward them from the creek.

Rebecca turned to keep the dog from shaking creek water all over her, but Lily Dog kept coming. Then next thing she knew, the dog ran around her leg and accidentally tripped her up, causing her to start a fast fall.

Right into Jeb's arms.

Cabbage and asparagus flew through the air.

Together, they stumbled and fell to the ground, Lily Dog dancing and barking all around them, enjoying this new game.

Becca hit his chest with a thump, her breath leaving her body. Then she glanced down at him, saw the need in his eyes, and felt that same need inside her heart.

"Becca," he said again. "I need—"

Rebecca pushed away, not daring to kiss him, although she wanted that badly. She pushed against the ground and managed to stand. Grabbing enough fresh asparagus to feed two, she said, "I'm going to make supper. You can stay or not. It's up to you."

"I'm staying," he said. "And Becca, I'm not just talking about staying for supper. I'm going to find a way to stay here in Campton Creek for the rest of my life."

Rebecca's heart lifted at that passionate declaration, but it sank fast when she thought of all the things still between them. "Biscuits or corn bread?" she asked, thinking she sounded *dumm.*

He blinked, got up and wiped his hands down his pants. "Biscuits sound *gut.* And I do like asparagus."

Rebecca marched to the house, thinking between his mixed signals and her constant state of confusion, it would take something big to ever bring them together.

Or something big to destroy both of them all over again.

Chapter Twenty

Jeb thought this would be the time to come clean, except he and Noah had agreed to wait until after Becca's birthday.

So now here he sat, his hair still damp from sticking his head under the cool pump water, his skin smelling like lemongrass and heather soap, watching Becca move around her kitchen. She'd barely spoken to him, but he heard her humming as she worked. Somehow, this felt right. Better than any of the places he'd worked and lived before.

He wished with all his heart he could have supper with her for the rest of his life. Surely, God hadn't brought him here and let him fall for this woman, just to have him leave again. He'd tell the bishop he was ready to go before the church. He knew in his heart he needed to be right here.

"That sure smells good," he said. "Do you need any help?"

She whirled, her expression showing he'd insulted her in some way. "I don't mind cooking for you, Jeb."

"I didn't mean you're not capable," he said, his tongue becoming tied. "I love your cooking. I guess I'm used to batching it, is all."

She finished checking on the steamed asparagus and then checked the baked chicken and rice in the oven. Wiping her hands down her apron, she fixed tea for them and came to sit at the table. "It will be ready in a few minutes."

Jeb took a sip of tea. "Franny brought me some tea the other day—tea with lemons, mint and honey. It was good."

"Would you rather I added those items?"

"Neh," he said, getting more flustered by the minute. "Why are you so mad at me?"

Rebecca looked sheepish. "I don't know. I don't want to be mad, but... I can't name why I'm feeling this way. I wanted us to have a nice dinner. I made a cake—strawberries and white cake with whipped cream."

"I like that kind of cake."

"Gut."

"I don't think you're mad at me, really," he said. "I think we're trying hard to not like each other, but Becca I do like you. A lot."

She stared over at him, her hands in her lap, her eyes as pretty as any forest he'd ever seen. "What are we to do, then?"

"We can continue as we've planned, and let God show us the way," he said, meaning it. Wanting it.

"I like that plan, and I'm sorry I've been...mad."

"Does that mean you care about me?"

She nodded, looked down at her hands. "I don't want you to feel obligated, Jeb."

"Obligated?" He couldn't believe she didn't see how much he'd fallen for her. Yet, he couldn't tell her that. Not yet.

"I know Noah has been pushing you toward me. It's pathetic that my brother is constantly trying to match me with anyone who comes along." She twisted her apron in her hands. "I told myself I'd just ignore him, and I even warned him to stop. He did seem to stop, but now you're acting strange and he's acting strange, and I know something is going on with you two. Is my brother hounding you about me? You don't have to sacrifice yourself for me. I can take care of myself. I've learned that. I will be okay."

He saw the tears she'd tried so hard to hold back. Jeb got up and lifted her out of her chair. "Becca," he said, taking her hands in his, his eyes on her, "no one is hounding me, and you are not pathetic.

You are one of the strongest women I've ever met. I've had every opportunity to marry—either Amish, Mennonite or *Englisch*. But none of them have compared to you, do you understand me?"

She bobbed her head and wiped at her eyes. "But I kissed you and messed things up—I was too bold and reckless."

Jeb shook his head. "I told you I liked kissing you."

"But—"

He stopped her, his nose lifting in the air. "But... I think something is burning."

She whirled and ran to the stove. "Your biscuits."

"*My* biscuits?"

She grabbed a potholder and opened the oven to grab the pan of slightly singed biscuits. "And the chicken and rice will be dry now."

"My biscuits," he repeated, a smile cresting his face. "You have burned my biscuits."

"This is not funny," she said, fussing

with getting the chicken and rice out. "I've ruined our meal."

He held a hand to his lip to keep from laughing.

"What is wrong with you?" she asked, glancing around.

"It's just between Old Billy ruining the Farmer's Daughters and you burning *my* biscuits, we seem to always be in trouble a lot, don't you think?"

Rebecca put her hands on her hips and tried to be mad. But instead of pouting, she started giggling. Then they both started laughing. Jeb came to her and grabbed her hands again, dancing her around the kitchen.

They stopped, both out of breath, and he looked into her eyes. "I like burned biscuits, Becca. I like the way you make me laugh. I haven't laughed this much in such a long time."

He held her there, savoring having her in his arms. Then he leaned over and whispered, "This is the part where you kiss me again."

She did kiss him again. When she finally pulled away, Jeb stepped back and smiled. "Don't ever think anyone feels sorry for you, Rebecca. I think everyone around here admires you. I know I do." Then he looked at the food. "And I can't wait to eat burned biscuits and dry chicken."

She slapped at his arm, but her smile countered that action. "Then help me get our food on the table and we will enjoy our messed-up meal."

Jeb smiled and helped her finish up. "Nothing with you is messed up," he said. "And just so you know, Noah has not been after me about marrying you. Other things, yes. But not that."

She gave him a puzzled glance. "Then what's wrong with both of you lately? You've avoided me and he's acting like a cat in a roomful of rocking chairs. What is he after you about now, Jeb?"

* * *

Jeb seemed to like the cake. She sent some home with him, watching him out the front door. She half expected Noah to *kumm* running with either a knowing grin or a stern frown. But her brother seemed subdued these days.

Rebecca was more confused than ever.

Jeb hadn't really told her anything to ease the nagging dread she felt in her heart. After her question, he only said that Noah liked to pick at him about almost everything, but that lately they'd been getting along a lot better.

So why had Jeb avoided her so much before their supper together?

True, they had been busy, and they couldn't stand around flirting while customers kept coming on a daily basis. Today, a whole bus full of tourists had arrived and they'd asked a lot of questions. She and Jeb, and sometimes Adam, had done their best to answer all the questions.

Now as she looked out over the yard and

fields, she could see all the improvements Jeb had helped her with. The barn looked fresh from a new coat of red paint. She knew it was in tip-top condition inside, too, since Adam went on and on about helping Jeb fix it up. She'd peeked in once or twice, but she still couldn't bring herself to go near the horses. It wasn't that she was so terrified of them, but the trauma of seeing John go flying through the air and then never waking up was just too much to remember all over again.

John.

She felt the guilt of not remembering him as much now. It had been so long, and yet, she didn't want to forget him. Jeb reminded her so much of him at times, she had to turn away. But Jeb was different, more confident, and older, strong, and dependable. John would have been all those things if he'd lived.

She had to stop comparing the two of them. It wasn't fair to Jeb. Since their dinner the other night, he'd been kind and considerate and he found ways to make her smile. He and Adam were *gut* at doing silly things to get her attention. Lily Dog always went along with the fun, causing all of them to giggle.

But Rebecca still had that feeling that something wasn't right. Maybe it was because she'd forgotten how it felt to be in love. She had fallen for Jeb. It was an easy fall, a soft, delicate drifting, as a leaf would let go of a tree and fall softly to earth. She couldn't come out and tell him, but he had to know. He had to feel her heart beating against his chest when he held her, he had to feel the warm intensity that flowed over her when he kissed her. He had to see it in her eyes each time he looked at her.

Especially after the burnt biscuits episode. She still giggled and got all dreamy— over biscuits! He'd eaten them with butter and declared they were the best biscuits ever.

That had to mean he loved her in some

small way. He just had a lot to work through to come to his own conclusions. But the bishop had stopped her at church the other day.

"Jeb is a *gut* man, Rebecca. I hope whatever his future holds, that he will stay here among us. I'm praying for you, and your part in that decision."

Bishop King never pushed, and he never made demands. He usually laid out how things should be and the consequences of anyone's actions if they strayed. Then he guided that person into making the best decision. He wanted Jeb to stay.

And so did she.

But Jeb and *Gott* would have to have that discussion.

She stood on the porch now, taking in the late afternoon sun that shifted in a golden glow across the trees and fields. Jeb had gone home, Adam trailing by his side, talking away about the snake they'd found and sent to the woods, and the big fish he'd seen jumping in the creek.

She loved hearing their conversations.

When she saw a shadow coming around the side of the house, her heart expected Jeb. But Franny waved to her and smiled.

"What brings you over?" Rebecca asked, thinking they'd done enough putting up and canning to last for years.

"I want to go into town Saturday afternoon," Franny said. "I thought you and Hannah might want to ride with me. It can be your birthday outing. Then when we get home, we can have a picnic supper out under the trees."

Surprised, Rebecca stared at her sister-in-law. "That's a lot for one day. We usually just have cake and punch."

"Oh, we'll have cake," Franny said. "I ordered one from Ava Jane Weaver."

"Oh, she makes the best cakes," Rebecca said, touched that Franny was being so kind. "You don't have to do this, you know."

Franny glanced around. "But I do. I mean I want to give you a special day.

You've worked hard and helped me with getting all the jellies and jams made, and the produce put away. We won't starve this winter. Let's have some fun, okay?"

"I really didn't want to dwell on my birthday."

"You won't dwell. You'll be having fun with your sisters."

Rebecca did consider Franny a sister, same as her real sister. "What does Hannah say?"

"She's excited to be included. We'll leave after you shut down for the day. I have meat for burgers and Noah said he'd help with preparations—something he rarely offers."

"A real picnic, for my birthday. I can bring a side dish."

"*Neh*, you are the birthday girl. You don't have to worry about anything."

Franny seemed so set on doing this, Rebecca couldn't refuse. "I will be ready after dinner hour," she said, smiling.

"*Denke*, Franny. This is so thoughtful, and it sounds like fun."

"*Gut*," Franny said. "No church on Sunday so we can rest up then."

Rebecca hugged her sister-in-law, then Franny took a glance at the lily field. "Oh, my, Rebecca. This looks so pretty with the late sun shining on it. You and Jeb have done wonders."

"Adam helped," she said, smiling. "This summer has been my best so far. I've had more customers than ever."

"You're so smart and I'm so happy for you," Franny replied. "You've helped me with the youngies so much. *Denke*."

Rebecca smiled. "I'm thankful to have you and Noah so close."

"And now you have help, *ja*?"

Rebecca chuckled. "Jeb is certainly strong and hardworking. Moses Yoder reminded me of a tortoise, but he did try."

Franny chatted a little more and picked out a pretty apricot-colored lily with curly, plush blooms. "Take it," Rebecca said. "On the house."

She waved her sister-in-law home, smiling as she thought of the fun day they'd have on Saturday.

Her life was settling into a nice, pleasant routine.

And Jeb had become a part of that routine. She only hoped her peace could last past summer.

Chapter Twenty-One

Saturday turned out to be a beautiful day, warm with a gentle breeze and blue skies for miles. The kind of day with many possibilities.

Jeb went through the morning eagerly awaiting the time when he and his friends would meet in Noah's barn to move wood slats, and then do the same in Rebecca's barn. They'd piece together the numbered boards to quickly build Rebecca's shed.

Jeb had made a sign for it—Rebecca's Lily Garden—that he hoped she'd like. Franny had painted a bright burgundy lily with a yellow throat on the small piece of wood. He'd hang it over the double doors that he'd already had Tobias Mast smooth and polish at the furniture shop where he worked. Noah had kept them in his barn and Tobias had come there to finish up his work. Just about everyone except Rebecca was in on this surprise.

He only hoped his grand plan wouldn't backfire on him.

The day passed with vehicles coming and going up and down the lane leading to the gardens and fields. Not only did they sell all the potted lilies, but Adam and Jeb had dug up a few and potted them on the spot. Rebecca patiently answered the many questions people asked, handing them one of the pamphlets Jeb and Jewel had created. They seemed to do the trick, especially since Jewel had added several good websites on growing lilies.

They needed to set up their own website, he thought as he hurried around to clean up everything and make sure the lilies hadn't been trampled by all the folks who'd been here.

A lot of their visitors only wanted pictures, so last week he and Adam had set out benches and made designated trails for the lookers to follow. He'd noticed several parents taking pictures of their children sitting on one of the benches, lilies blooming like a rainbow in every color behind them.

He thought of the bench by the creek, smiling when he remembered being there with Rebecca. Maybe after today, after they'd celebrated her birthday, she'd see that he cared for her deeply. And she'd understand why he hadn't been honest with her.

He was headed toward the barn with the wheelbarrow when he heard her calling.

"Jeb?"

Jeb set down the wheelbarrow and turned to greet her. She'd changed her work dress for a mint green fresh frock and a crisp white apron. She looked so pretty as she walked toward him.

"*Ja?*"

"I'm about to leave with Franny and Hannah for our town trip." She gave him a shy smile. "Are you coming to the gathering later?"

"Oh, you mean, will I be at your birthday celebration?"

"It's not a celebration, just people getting together. Family."

He wondered if he would be part of her family one day.

"I plan to. I wouldn't miss it."

"You want cake, right?"

"Right. That's why I want to be there."

Her eyes lit up while her smile shot hope straight to his heart. "I'll be back in a few hours. Try to stay out of trouble."

"I will," he said, his heart beating so fast, he had to take a deep breath. "You do the same."

She laughed and waved, looking so young and happy, his guilt kicked at him like an old mule. He would hate to destroy that happiness.

A few minutes later, Noah and the crew showed up. Adam came running toward the barn. "Are you ready, Jeb?"

"I'm so ready," Jeb said, waving to Jeremiah Weaver, Tobias Mast, Josiah Fisher and Micah King.

"We have others on the way," Jeremiah said, ready to get to work. "But we can get the framework set up."

Jeb nodded and showed them where the slats and boards had been hidden in the back of the barn. Noah and his sons went back to his place to load everything they had hidden there.

Soon the fields echoed with hammering and men shouting and talking. Jeb stopped and glanced around, making sure no women were approaching.

He wanted this to be the best surprise Rebecca had ever had. And the best birthday.

Franny held tightly to the buggy reins, occasionally turning to check on Rebecca in the back, while Hannah rode up front with her. "How ya doing back there?"

"I'm okay, Franny," Rebecca said. "I know you're a *wunderbar gut* driver."

"And I'm right here," Hannah said, smiling over her shoulder. "This was such a sweet idea, Franny. I haven't been on a girls' outing in so long."

"Noah suggested it," Franny said. "He's getting mellow in his old age."

"Wait," Rebecca said, leaning up. "Did you say my brother suggested this?"

Franny checked the reins, but she looked *ferhoodled*. "I mean, he asked if I'd like to take you both into town. Just a thought."

Rebecca smiled at her sister-in-law's confusion, but she got that feeling inside that something was off. Why would she think that just because her brother and his wife were thinking of her on a special day?

"That was thoughtful of our *bruder*," Hannah said.

At least she hadn't been acting strange.

But then, no one told Hannah their secrets. Rebecca was surprised her sweet but talkative sister hadn't blabbed about Rebecca's feelings regarding Jeb.

"I thought we'd start with a quick bite at the Campton Creek Café," Franny said. "It's that new place that Jewel and some of our friends have opened. A lot of Amish are employed there. Jewel helps when she can, but she has her hands full with the Campton Center."

"That would be nice," Rebecca said. "But I must save room for supper tonight, too."

Hannah grinned. "I'm hungry already." She looked so shy, Rebecca now had to worry about her, too. What was she hiding?

Franny parked the buggy across from the new café, secured the horses and marched them across the street. The café was in what used to be a small Victorian-style house. It was past lunch hour, so they found a nice table on the big porch where they could sit in the shade of an aged oak tree.

Once they were seated, Rebecca glanced at her sister. "Hannah, are you feeling poorly? You're pale today."

Hannah shook her head. "*Neh*, I mean... I'm feeling a little faint is all." She took a sip of the water a young Amish girl had brought them. "I'm feeling...different."

Franny stared at Hannah and then put a hand to her mouth. "Are you with child?"

Rebecca glanced at Hannah, and then she saw her sister's apologetic eyes. "You're expecting?"

Hannah nodded. "I didn't want to spoil your day, but I'm a little shaky. I need food."

Rebecca got up and came around the table to hug her sister. "Why would you worry about me? You know I'm thrilled for you."

"Are you?" Hannah asked. "I was afraid...it would make you sad."

Rebecca touched a hand to Hannah's

face. "Silly, I'm happy. I will be the first to spoil this child."

Hannah hugged her tight. "I'm so glad you're okay with this. I...miss Mamm so much right now."

Franny got up to hug her, too. "You have us, sister. We will pamper both you and the *bobbeli*."

The waitress came back, concern on her face. "Can I help?"

"We're fine," Franny said, a smile on her face as she wiped her eyes. "We are celebrating a newcomer to our family."

The girl clapped her hands together. "We have cupcakes. I'll bring a big one for dessert."

Rebecca laughed and nodded. "We'll let the expecting mother eat most of it."

They ordered salads and laughed and talked.

Rebecca kept smiling at her little sister. A new baby for her to spoil. She couldn't wait to tell Jeb.

That thought made her heart burn with

a need she had tried to hide. She wished she could experience having a child of her own. But she prayed for God's guidance and wisdom.

Being married to Jeb would be more than enough.

Three hours later, Jeb stood back and smiled.

"We did it, Jeb," Adam said, slapping Jeb on the back. "It looks real pretty, too."

"It does look nice," Jeb replied, ruffling Adam's hair.

"I need some water and a snack," Adam said. "I'm tired."

The other men had left for home. Now Jeb had to get cleaned up for supper at Noah's house. But first, he wanted to finish cleaning up things around here. Becca should be home before sundown, so he wanted to be here when she spotted the fresh new shed near the old oak. He'd found an old wooden picnic table at a garage sale a couple of weeks ago and taken it to the Furniture Mart in town where Tobias worked. Together, they'd spruced it up and Tobias had brought it today.

Now, it was centered off to the side of the shed with a potted lily—a Farmer's Daughter—sitting on the table.

He finished up, pleased that everything was coming together. The minute he saw the buggy returning from town, he'd walk over and ask Rebecca to come back here with him for just a few minutes.

He'd get through today, and his gift to her. Then tomorrow, he'd tell her the last of his secrets.

"We are running out of room."

Franny and Hannah laughed as Rebecca tried to find a spot for all the bags and boxes they'd loaded into the buggy.

"But we have so much—our fabrics for dresses and quilts, more jam jars for canning, some new books to read. Did I miss anything?" Franny asked, laughing.

"I need to run into the general store,"

Rebecca said. "I remembered I need some more pots. We've used so many more this season. I can buy up what is in stock and order a new shipment through Mr. Hartford and get a discount."

"Okay, I'll go in with you," Franny said. "I'm sure I can find something I need."

Hannah got out of the buggy and sat on a bench out front. She had grown tired. "I'll be here, napping like an old man."

Franny and Rebecca hurried in and headed back to the garden section. Franny went one way and Rebecca went the other.

Rebecca was trying to decide how many pots to order and which colors when she ran into Shem Yoder. He and Moses were related in some way, but she rarely saw the reclusive widower.

Smiling, she said, "Hello, Shem. I haven't seen you in a while."

The older man stared at her. "Rebecca?"

"That's me," she said, thinking he'd aged a lot.

"I was just thinking about you the other

day," he replied, his face squinting into a grimace. "You and John—so sad that."

She blinked, surprised to hear that coming out of his mouth. Nodding, she turned back to her pots. But Shem kept standing there. "Did you need something, Shem?"

He scratched his beard. "Minna had a sister, Moselle."

Confused, Rebecca nodded. "Yes, John's *mamm* had a sister named Minna, but she moved away before I ever met her."

"Minna married a Martin," Shem went on. "John's cousin sure looks just like him, ain't so?"

Rebecca thought she'd heard wrong. "What did you say?"

Shem's eyes widened and he turned so quickly, he almost knocked over a shelf full of gadgets.

"Shem, are you all right?"

Shem looked confused. "You know, the man who works for you." Then he put a hand to his mouth. "I'm sorry. I've said too much."

He lifted his hat and slowly walked away, leaving Rebecca so shocked, she dropped the plastic flowerpot she was holding.

John's cousin looks just like him, ain't so?

You know, the man who works for you.

Rebecca couldn't move. John's cousin? Martin. Minna Martin. Jeb Martin.

Franny came rushing toward her. "Becca, what happened?"

Rebecca grabbed her sister-in-law's hand. "I need to get home."

"Are you ill?" Franny asked as she reached down to pick up the cracked pot.

Rebecca held a hand to her head. "*Neh*, but I need to talk to Jeb. Right now."

Franny set the pot back on the table and took her toward the front door. "We'll pay for the busted flowerpot later, Mr. Hartford," she told the surprised owner. "Becca isn't feeling well right now."

Rebecca could barely get into the buggy. Her hands were shaking, and a cold sweat inched down her spine. Hannah kept asking what had happened, but Franny just shook her head.

Rebecca sank back on her seat, her stomach roiling and lurching with each bump of the buggy.

Could it be true? Could Jeb be John's cousin?

And if so, why hadn't he told her that from the beginning?

Chapter Twenty-Two

Jeb saw the buggy coming up the lane, his emotions going from relief to gratitude to happiness and back to fear and doubt. What if Becca didn't like surprises? What if she hated the shed? Then, would she ever forgive him when he explained things to her?

As Franny trotted the horses to the barn, everyone waiting for them waved. Hannah's husband had arrived, and he was all grins. Noah and the boys tried to stand still, but Adam was hopping from foot to foot. And Katie, who'd pouted most of the day for not being able to go with the women, went running to the buggy.

"You're home," she shouted. "Did you bring me some candy, Mamm?"

Franny hopped down, her eyes on Noah. She motioned to him.

Jeb saw Rebecca and started heading toward them, but she glanced up, got down from the buggy and took off toward her house.

"What's wrong?" Noah asked, while Hannah hurried Katie toward the house, her husband, Samuel, hurrying after her.

Franny glanced toward Rebecca's house. "I don't know. She was talking to Shem Yoder in the general store, and she looked so...shocked. She wanted to come home immediately."

Noah sent Jeb a knowing glare. "We knew this would happen. Now what are you going to do?"

Jeb knew what he had to do, and he also knew it was all over now. He'd have to leave. If Shem had told her the truth, Rebecca would never forgive him.

Franny's gaze moved from him to Jeb. "What are you talking about?"

Noah motioned to Jeb. "Go after her."

Then he took Franny by the arm. "I'll explain everything."

"*Ja*, you will," his wife said. "I've never seen Rebecca so shattered. At least not since John died."

Jeb took a deep breath, went inside the *grossdaddi haus* and found the letters from John. Then he walked up the lane to Rebecca's house. It was the hardest walk he'd ever made.

Rebecca made it as far as the kitchen, where she sank down on a chair and held a hand to her mouth. It all made sense now, of course. Jeb looked so much like John. She'd seen that, felt that in her heart. But she'd decided she just missed John and she'd imagined the rest. How silly, how naive she'd been.

When she heard a knock at the front door, that day she'd seen Jeb walking up the lane the first time came back to her. She wouldn't allow him into her house again, and she'd get him out of her heart. Somehow.

"Becca." He called her name like a plea. "I'm so sorry. I wanted to tell you a thousand times, but I had an excuse for not telling you—any excuse I could find. I didn't know, Becca. I didn't know until you told me your name. And by then, I didn't want to go. I wanted this job and later after we'd worked together and I got to know you and your family, and this community, I wanted to stay here with you forever."

Rebecca gulped a sob, her head falling into her hands. She'd never been betrayed in such a cruel way. Never. This hurt almost as much as losing John.

"Becca, please. I… I have letters from John. I'll let you see them. I wanted to tell you so many times."

Letters? He had letters from the man

she was meant to be with, the man she'd longed for all these years. All this time, he'd had letters. Every time she'd mentioned John, Jeb had known. He'd known what he was doing.

She sat, her hands shaking, her lungs burning, her eyes streaming silent tears— tears of grief, anger, disbelief and heartache.

She was living it all over again because she'd trusted a man who reminded her so much of John.

John was in heaven.

Jeb was here on earth.

In her whole life, she'd only loved two men.

One she'd never forget, and one she'd never forgive.

She got up and went upstairs and fell across her bed.

Then she remembered it was her birthday, and the tears came all over again. Her heart hurt so badly, she felt the burn of it all the way to her soul.

There was no getting over this. Ever.

* * *

Jeb didn't know what to do. She wouldn't open the door, so he went around back. He didn't try to go up on the porch or into the house. Instead, he took the bundle of letters to the new shed, the smell of fresh wood and lilies merging around him with what seemed like a taunting scent.

What have I done?

He stood in the shed, praying to the Lord. Asking for true forgiveness, from the Master. Asking for redemption from the One who could give it. He'd do anything to make this up to Rebecca. Anything.

Even leaving her if that's what it would take.

But he didn't want to leave. He wanted to comfort her and hold her and tell her how much he loved her. He'd fallen for her the moment he'd seen her. Before he even knew her name.

He should have left then, after he'd figured things out. But coward that he was, he'd stayed and withheld the most important thing he could tell her. Now, she'd heard it from an old man who got confused, but who also had a memory that seemed as sharp as ever. He couldn't blame this on Shem, though. The man knew what he knew. And so did Jeb. But Shem told the truth in his misguided way.

Jeb had held the truth away because he didn't want to wander anymore. Now he'd have to do that very thing anyway.

He stood in the little building he'd created to show Rebecca how much he cared. Turning, he stared up at the house for a long time, hoping she'd come outside.

But the sun began to set, and she still hadn't opened any doors. Jeb left the letters there on the small counter he'd made for her. Then he turned and headed for the barn. He'd make sure the animals were taken care of for tonight at least. Because he'd be gone by morning's light.

* * *

Rebecca heard someone knocking at the back door.

Groggy and confused, she sat up and realized she'd fallen asleep with her clothes on. Outside, the sunset shot ribbons of purple and gold across the lily field. She went to the window and looked down, thinking Jeb was back. The whole place looked like a painting—a painting done by the Master, the One who watched over even the lilies of the field.

Then she noticed the shed.

How was this possible? There had been no shed there when she'd left all those hours ago. Her heart hammered the answer while she tried to ignore it.

Jeb. It had to have been Jeb.

When she saw her brother walking away from the house, she hurried down and came out the front door, so she could speak to him about the new building on her property. And about Jeb.

"Noah."

Her brother whirled as she called from the front porch. "There you are. We were fearsome worried about you."

Rebecca straightened her *kapp* and wiped at her tear-swollen eyes. "Were you worried when Jeb told you the truth?"

Noah looked so guilty, she almost felt sorry for him. "Why didn't you say something? You were the one who warned me against him."

"I only found out a few weeks ago, not all of it, mind you. But Shem had put things together and asked around. I came to Jeb and confronted him. He told me the rest—about John."

Her anger returned, burning like lightning down her stomach. "You should have told me."

"It wasn't my place, Becca," he said, his hands out. "Jeb promised me he'd tell you everything—after your birthday."

She sank down on a rocking chair. "Why would it matter which day he told me?"

"He wanted... He made you a gift..."

Noah stopped. "The man is in love with you, Becca."

As much as those words jolted her heart, she couldn't accept that now. "Well, he has a funny way of showing it—keeping this secret from me the whole time, Noah. The times we worked together, laughed together, chased your goat, ran off deer, every little thing we did together, and he knew, he knew how much this would hurt me."

Noah came to her and patted her shoulder, tears in his eyes. "He did know this would hurt you, sister. He fought with it day and night. He told the bishop and Bishop King urged him to be truthful with you. Jeb was afraid it would destroy you."

"Well, Jeb was right," she said. "I don't know if I can ever get over this."

"But he built you a garden shed."

"That won't help my broken heart," she replied. "Nothing can help that."

Noah nodded and stood. Then he said,

"Katie is asking after you. She wants you to have your birthday party."

"I ruined the day for her, didn't I?"

"We explained that you felt ill," he said. "Hannah and Samuel entertained her. Hannah wanted to come and check on you, but I told her I'd do it. We can celebrate another day."

"Tell Hannah to go home. She needs her rest. Or did you know that secret, too?"

Noah shook his head. "She told me a little while ago. Oh, and Adam came over to help Jeb in the barn. I think the boy wanted to find out what was going on. He sure was looking forward to you seeing that shed. We all helped build it. Jeb mapped out the pieces and had it all planned out. We had us a regular shed-raising while you were in town."

"I suppose everyone was in on that, too," she said, her heart too bruised to thank him.

"*Ja*, because we all love you and because we thought—"

"Don't say it." She stood. "I'm going to check on the lilies and then I'm going to bed."

"But it's almost dark."

"I'll just stand on the porch and make sure the fields are quiet."

She watched her brother walking away, then turned and went inside. There was just enough light left for her to go out to that shed and have one look at it. Before she told her brother to tear it down.

Jeb pivoted when the barn door creaked open, hoping Rebecca had come to talk to him. But when Adam stuck his head in, Jeb swallowed his disappointment. Only because the boy looked so dejected. Lily Dog pushed past Adam and ran up to Jeb, barking hello. Jeb rubbed the dog's head.

"Hey, Jeb," Adam said as he moved up the short stable alley, petting Red and Silver as he walked by. "Is Rebecca feeling better? Did she see her shed yet? Is she gonna be okay?"

Jeb swallowed again. "She's still not feeling well, so I think she went to bed. She'll have to see her shed another day."

Adam's dejection held him like a heavy cloak. "We didn't even get to cut the cake and it's a mighty big cake, round and with a lot of high layers. And white icing with sprinkles and Ava Jane even put little flowers on there, like lilies and petunias or something. Things women like, I reckon. Katie's pouting about not getting her piece."

Jeb couldn't look at Adam. He was too ashamed. Darkness shrouded the barn, but he didn't want to leave this shelter. He reached for a kerosene lamp and lit it with the long matches he kept nearby, then set it on the table. The glow from the lamp showed Adam's confusion.

Adam came closer. "Jeb, are you disappointed that Aenti Becca didn't see her pretty garden shed?"

Jeb nodded, cleared his throat. "I am. But I'm more disappointed in myself."

"Why?" Adam asked, moving to help him put away the scrap lumber they'd saved from the shed building. Lily Dog ran back and forth, wondering what to do next.

Jeb was close to telling the boy the truth about why Rebecca was feeling so bad, but when he turned to face Adam, he accidentally tripped over an extended four-by-four board he'd leaned against the worktable. The table wobbled and the kerosene lamp fell to the floor, landing against some old rags and a pile of straw. Jeb lost his footing and his balance. He went down hard, hitting his head against the thick wooden board. He landed, blinked and saw stars. Then he saw fire running up the wall, before everything went black.

Chapter Twenty-Three

Rebecca stood in the shed, amazed at how beautiful it was. It smelled fresh and clean. New. Two small windows on each side allowed for airflow when opened and…also allowed for seeing both the sunrise to the east and the sunset to the west on most days. The little work counter and the stool behind it were both perfect, and so was the potting table spreading the length of one wall, complete with tools hanging over it and baskets and pots sitting on a rack below. The picnic table off to the side held a lily she recognized immediately. The Farmer's Daughter. Its bright pink petals and soft yellow throat shined against the sunrays covering the yard. How could she forget that day? How could she forget this summer?

But when she spotted the stack of letters tied with a string of twine lying there on the counter, her heartbeat went into a rapid retreat. Jeb had left her the letters from John.

She stood and took it all in, thinking of what might have been if he'd been honest with her.

And how would she have reacted? Would she have accepted him and let it all fall into place? Or would she have turned him away, her heart still broken over losing her childhood sweetheart? She'd never know because Jeb had not given her that choice. How she wished he would have trusted her enough to be honest with her. Knowing he was John's cousin should bring her comfort, but now it only brought her another kind of horrible pain. The pain of feeling betrayed by a man she'd learned to trust.

What am I to do now, Lord?

Then she heard the dog barking—an urgent, swift bark that sounded different. Rebecca turned, the smell of smoke rising through the air. When she heard a scream coming from the barn, she rushed out the door, Lily Dog barking and twirling in front of her. The dog wanted her to go to the barn.

Her breath gasping, her feet taking her forward, Rebecca cringed and put a hand to her mouth. The barn was on fire.

She glanced around, thinking no one was here to help her. But she'd heard a scream. She heard it again.

"Aenti!"

Adam. Adam was in the barn.

Had Jeb already left?

When she heard one of the horses whinnying in a panic, she knew she had to save Adam—and Red and Silver, too. Asking God to give her strength, she pushed at the half-open door and stood staring as fire licked the back wall with a hungry anger. Then she saw Adam tugging on something.

"Adam?"

"Aenti, it's Jeb." Her nephew's hoarse, breathless shouts sent a cold sweat across her skin. "He tripped over a board and the lamp fell. He got knocked out. Help!"

Jeb. She had to save Jeb.

She rushed forward. She and Adam tried to get him up, but the big board that had fallen kept him wedged between the table and the dirt floor.

"The horses," Adam called. "We have to drag him away." Her nephew started coughing again.

She couldn't let Adam stay here. The fire was spreading too fast, its golden flames sparking and flashing heat over their heads.

"Adam, go and get your *daed*. Hurry. I'll get the horses out and I'll find a way to get Jeb."

"*Neh*, I can't leave you."

"Just go. Now. Run fast. We need help."

Adam gave her one last panicked glance, then hurried out the door. Lily Dog ran with him.

Rebecca lifted her apron over her nose, then searched for a rope. Finding what she needed, she kept an eye on the fire behind the worktable. She had to get to the horses and use one to drag Jeb out. Or he would die.

"I can't let that happen," she shouted. "I can't go through this again."

She loved him. She knew in her heart, she loved him. No matter what, she couldn't let him go.

Right now, she didn't dwell on his misguided deceit. She only wanted Jeb to live. So she dropped her apron and pulled her *kapp* down like a mask, then went to Red and let her out. The roan rushed past her, scaring her almost as much as the fire. Then she found Silver, the gentle draft. Silver, the stronger of the two, would cooperate, she hoped. Grabbing the bit and reins next to the stall, she prayed for God to give her the courage she needed to help Jeb. While the fire clawed its way to the ceiling, she opened the stall and threw an old blanket over the draft's head, then guided him back to where Jeb lay. So still. So quiet.

"Jeb, please wake up."

He didn't move. She'd have to use the rope to tie his feet, but she didn't have time to get the reins and bit onto the horse. She'd have to guide Silver out by coaxing the horse and walking with him.

Rushing around, she steadied the horse with calm words, and threw a rope around Silver's middle, looped it back through to cinch it, then tugged the length of the rope toward Jeb. Silver whinnied and tossed his head back but didn't run away. After tying Jeb's feet, her hands shaking and her fingers working swiftly, Rebecca managed to secure the rope across his work boots. She touched his neck, searching for a pulse.

He was breathing. Somehow, she had to make this horse help her get Jeb to safety.

* * *

With a tug and all the strength she had, Rebecca got the heavy beam of wood moved enough to drag Jeb away without hurting him more. When she saw blood near his temple, she went into full panic mode.

"Silver, I know you can do this. You're a *gut* boy." She kept talking in soothing terms to the frightened horse while she tugged at the lasso around the animal's big girth. Clicking her tongue the way her *daed* used to do, she held the blanket over Silver's head and urged the horse forward, her prayers centered on saving Jeb, instead of fearing she'd get knocked out by the horse.

Silver's fear increased as the smell of smoke and the heat from the fire leaping behind them caused him to balk and lift up his massive front legs.

Rebecca stepped away, her heart dropping. "C'mon, Silver. We can do this. We have to do this. I need to tell him I love him, I forgive him. I don't want him to die."

Silver neighed a high-pitched whine, but when the horse heard voices coming from the yard, he bolted forward, almost knocking Rebecca down. Rebecca stepped back, watching as the rope she'd tied to Jeb's feet held enough for him to come flying up the alleyway.

"No," she shouted, her hands gripping the heavy rope. If the horse went too fast, Jeb would be dragged and hurt even worse. "Silver," she shouted, "wait."

Tugging at the rope with all her might, Rebecca managed to control the nervous animal, her hands burning from the heat and from the rope searing into her palms. But she couldn't let go. Silver practically dragged both Rebecca and Jeb out of the open door.

Then before she knew what was happening, her brother and his three sons surrounded her and took the rope from her.

"Becca, let me," Noah shouted, taking her hand away. "Go, get out of here."

Becca looked into her brother's eyes and then she looked at Jeb. "Don't let him die, Noah."

Adam guided her out into the night air. Gasping, she didn't realize she'd been holding her breath—but not against the smoke. *Neh*, she'd been holding steady for Jeb's sake.

Franny came running and tugged her to the picnic table. The table Jeb had set up for her with the pretty lily centered on it.

Rebecca held to her sister-in-law. "Franny, he can't die. I can't let him die. I have to tell him I love him."

Franny held her tight. "He won't die. He won't. You saved him, Becca."

Katie ran to her mother. "Aenti, don't cry. It's okay. We saved the cake, too."

Becca laughed and took her niece onto her lap. Then she cried all over again, and she and Franny sat and prayed silent prayers while the volunteer fire department came and tried to save the barn.

When the paramedic walked by, Franny ran to one of them. "What about the man in the barn? My sister-in-law Rebecca needs to know if he's going to be okay."

The paramedic nodded and motioned to Rebecca. "Why don't you go see for yourself. He's been asking for you."

Rebecca hurried to the stretcher they were about to lift into the ambulance. "Jeb?"

He groaned and turned his head. "You're here."

"I'm here," she said, taking his hand. "Jeb, I forgive you. I love you. I'm sorry."

She saw the tears in his eyes, saw the bump over his left temple. "Don't die on me."

"I'm not going to die," he said, his words weak. "I have so much to live for now. I hope you like your shed."

She started crying, her hand touching

his smut-covered face. "I love my shed. I love you. I'm sorry."

"*Neh*, I'm the one who's sorry, but, Becca, I love you so much."

Rebecca watched as they lifted him into the ambulance.

"He's going to be fine," Noah told her. "He has a slight concussion and a twisted ankle. You saved his life, Becca."

"And he saved mine," she replied.

A week later

Rebecca stood near the lily field, taking in a thousand scents while up at the house her belated birthday celebration was going strong.

Noah had finally cooked their hamburgers over a firepit grill that Mr. Hartford had sold him. They had potato salad, fresh cucumbers and several other side dishes. Franny had stored the cake at the Campton Center in a big freezer. Jewel had picked it up and kept it there until they were ready.

Today, they were all ready to celebrate. Jewel, with her usual energy, had helped with the whole gathering.

The neighbors had pitched in to rebuild the part of the barn that had burned. It looked new and fresh and strong. Rebecca could step inside now, her old fears burned away with the fire. Silver and she had a new beginning, a bond that brought them together.

A few days ago, Jeb had returned from the hospital, thanks to Jewel picking him up and bringing him home. He'd been resting so his foot and his head could heal. But today, he was well and at home for good.

Home. This would be his official home come this fall.

He'd told Becca in the hospital that he loved her and wanted to marry her.

"But we won't make it official until we're back home," he'd said, after he'd apologized over and over.

"Jeb, I was so angry at you, but I can understand why you did what you did. I loved John and I wasn't ready to let go of him. There was no easy way for you to tell me the truth."

She'd read the letters that night after the fire, and she'd cried with each word. But they had become a gift to her, a gift from the man she'd lost, brought to her by fate, from a man she'd found. She loved both of them.

One man in heaven.

One here on earth.

"What are you thinking?"

She turned as Jeb walked up to her and took her hand.

"I'm thinking about everything. About us, about the future, about the past. I'm so thankful for all of it."

He pulled her close. "I was an idiot."

"I was a bitter *alte maidal.*"

"We make a *gut* pair, right?"

"I believe so."

He glanced at the new shed and then back to her. "Becca, will you marry me?"

"Ja," she said, smiling, happy, glad.

"Okay, then. This fall. Meantime, I'm free and clear and I'm Amish again."

"That you are," she replied.

He'd stood up in church just yesterday and confessed all of his sins, including his connection to John.

He was forgiven. They would never speak of this again.

Rebecca wondered about all those who had to constantly pray for forgiveness. She sure had to do her own praying.

But now, she was content and at peace, and she thanked God for his perfect timing.

Only one thing held back her joy.

"I can't give you children, Jeb. I wonder how you feel about that."

Jeb turned her in his arms and kissed her. Then he drew back and smiled. "I'll tell you how I feel about that. *Gott*'s will, Becca. It took me twenty years to find you. We'll just have to see if he has one more blessing planned for us."

"You think?"

"I hope and pray, but if not, then I will still be the happiest man here on earth."

She nodded, unable to speak.

Then Katie and Lily Dog ran up.

"We really need to cut that cake, Aenti Becca. Please?"

"Please?" Jeb echoed.

Lily Dog barked.

Then they all walked together to join the rest of their family as the sun settled over the lily field and the air smelled like a wedding garden.

The Lily Lady had never been happier.

They were married in September, and a week before Christmas of the next year, they had a beautiful, healthy baby boy and named him John.

* * * * *

I hope wherever you are and whatever you might be going through in life, you

Dear Reader,

One of my favorite hymns is "In the Garden." Years ago, I wrote three Love Inspired books based on that hymn, *When Love Came to Town, Something Beautiful* and *Lacey's Retreat*. I loved describing the gardens in those books. My mama was a gardener and her flowers and plants brought her a lot of joy, so whenever I hear or sing that hymn where Jesus walks with us in the garden, I always think of her.

I love lilies, and not just daylilies, but lush, fragrant beautiful lilies of all colors and varieties. So it was a true joy to write about Rebecca, the Lily Lady, who tended her plants and grieved the man she'd lost. But God had a plan for Rebecca and so He brought Jebediah to her and showed her the true meaning of forgiveness and getting over tremendous grief. Jebediah had his secrets, but he had to learn to trust in God again to be able to confess his secrets and his love to Rebecca.

I hope wherever you are and whatever you might be going through in life, you will take some time to admire God's beautiful earth. Stop and smell the lilies. Now I want to plant a lot of lilies in my yard. Nature has a way of making even the worst of times better. I hope you find a flower today and I hope you know that He walks with you, and talks with you, wherever you are.

Until next time, may the angels watch over you. Always!

Lenora Worth